The
GOOD LITTLE DEVIL
AND OTHER TALES

Pushkin Children's Books
71–75 Shelton Street
London, WC2H 9JQ

Original Text © Éditions de la Table Ronde, Paris, 1967
Illustrated by Puig Rosado
Illustrations © Gallimard Jeunesse 1980
Translation © Sophie Lewis 2013

This edition published by Pushkin Children's Books in 2013

ISBN 978-1-78269-008-5

ROYAUME-UNI

This book is supported by the Institut français Royaume-
Uni as part of the Burgess programme
(www.frenchbooknews.com)

Set in 12 on 19 Berling Nova by Tetragon, London

Printed and bound in Italy by Printer Trento S.r.l.
on Munken Print White 100gsm

www.pushkinpress.com

The
GOOD LITTLE
DEVIL

AND OTHER TALES

by Pierre Gripari

Illustrated by Puig Rosado

Translated from the French by Sophie Lewis

PUSHKIN CHILDREN'S BOOKS

Contents

The Witch of Rue Mouffetard

There was once an old witch living in the Gobelins neighbourhood in Paris; she was a dreadfully old and ugly witch, but she really did want to be the most beautiful girl in the world!

One sunny day, while reading the *Witches' Times*, she came across the following advertisement:

MADAME
You who are OLD and UGLY
You shall become YOUNG and PRETTY!
To achieve this:
EAT A LITTLE GIRL
In tomato sauce!

Underneath, in small letters, it said:

Now, a little girl whose name was Nadia happened to be living in the very same neighbourhood as the witch. She was the eldest daughter of Papa Sayeed (perhaps you know him?), who kept the cafe-grocer's on rue Broca.

"I shall have to eat Nadia," the witch decided.

One fine day, Nadia had gone out to get some bread from the bakery when an old lady stopped and spoke to her:

"Good morning, young Nadia!"

"Good morning, madame!"

"Would you like to do me a good turn?"

"What is it?"

"Would you go and fetch a tin of tomato sauce from your daddy's shop for me? It would save me going, and I'm so tired today!"

Nadia agreed right away; she was a good-hearted

girl. As soon as she had gone, the witch—for it was she—began to laugh and rub her hands together:

"Oh, I am so cunning!" she said. "Young Nadia is going to bring me the very sauce that I shall eat her with!"

As soon as she had come back home with the bread, Nadia took a tin of tomato sauce from the shelves, and she was just getting ready to go out again when her father stopped her:

"And where are you off to, with that?"

"I am taking this tin of tomato sauce to an old lady who asked me for it."

"You stay here," said Papa Sayeed. "If your old lady wants something, she has only to come here herself."

Nadia, being also a very obedient girl, did not argue. But the next day, while out shopping, she was stopped by the old lady once again:

"Well, Nadia? What about my tomato sauce?"

"Sorry," said Nadia, blushing from head to foot, "but my daddy didn't want me to bring it. He said you should come to the shop yourself."

"Very well," said the old lady, "I'll come, then."

Indeed, she walked into the shop that very same day:

"Good morning, Monsieur Sayeed."

"Good morning, madame. What can I get you?"

"I would like Nadia."

"Excuse me?"

"Oh, forgive me! I meant to say: a tin of tomato sauce, please."

"Of course! A small one or a large one?"

"A large one, it's for Nadia..."

"What?"

"No, no! I meant to say: it's to have with some spaghetti..."

"I see! Talking of which, we also have spaghetti..."

"Oh, there's no need, I'll have Nadia..."

"What?"

"Do forgive me! I meant to say: the spaghetti, I already have some at home..."

"If you're sure... Here is your tomato sauce."

The old lady took the tin and paid for it, but then, instead of leaving, she began to look doubtful:

"Hm! Perhaps it is a little heavy... Do you think you might perhaps..."

"Might what?"

"Let Nadia carry it home for me?"

But Papa Sayeed had his suspicions.

"No, madame, we don't deliver. Besides, Nadia has other things to be getting on with. If this tin is too heavy for you, well, too bad: you'll just have to leave it behind!"

"Never mind," said the witch, "I'll take it. Goodbye, Monsieur Sayeed!"

"Goodbye, madame!"

And the witch went away, with her tin of tomato sauce. As soon as she was home, she said to herself:

"Here's an idea: tomorrow morning, I shall disguise myself as a butcher, then go to rue Mouffetard and sell some meat in the market. When Nadia comes out to do the shopping for her parents, I'll nab her."

The following day, the witch appeared on rue Mouffetard disguised as a market butcher, when Nadia happened to go by.

"Hello, little girl. Would you like some meat?"

"Oh no, madame, I've just bought a chicken."

"Shoot!" thought the witch.

Next day, back in the market, she had disguised herself as a poultry butcher.

"Hello, dear. Will you buy one of my chickens?"

"Oh no, madame. Today I'm looking for some red meat."

"Blast!" thought the witch.

On the third day, in a fresh disguise, she was selling both red meat and poultry.

"Hello Nadia, hello my dear! What would you like? You see, today I have something for everyone: beef, mutton, chicken, rabbit..."

"Yes, but we're having fish today!"

"Drat!"

Back at home, the witch thought and thought. Then she had a new idea:

"Well, if this is how things are, I will use some stronger magic. Tomorrow morning I shall turn myself into EVERY SINGLE ONE of the food-sellers on rue Mouffetard AT THE SAME TIME!"

And indeed, the following day, the witch had turned into every single one of the food-sellers on rue Mouffetard (there were exactly 267 of them), in disguise.

Nadia came along as usual and, quite unsuspecting, went up to a vegetable stall—to buy some green

15

beans, this time—and was about to pay when the shopkeeper caught her by the wrist, snatched her away and *ker-CHING*! shut her up in the till.

Luckily, Nadia had a little brother whose name was Bashir. Noticing that his big sister had not come home, Bashir said to himself:

"That witch must have taken her. I have to go and save her."

He picked up his guitar and headed off to rue Mouffetard. Seeing him approach, the 267 food-sellers (remember: every single one of them was actually the witch) began to call out:

"Where are you off to like that, Bashir?"

Bashir closed his eyes tight and answered:

"I am a poor blind musician; all I want is to sing a little song and earn myself a few pennies."

"What song?" the food-sellers asked.

"I want to sing a song called: *Nadia, Where Are You?*"

"No, not that one! Sing another!"

"But I don't know another song!"

"Then sing it really softly!"

"All right! I'll sing it really softly."

And Bashir began to sing as loudly as he could:

Nadia, where are you?
Nadia, where are you?
Reply so I can spy you!
Nadia, where are you?
Nadia, where are you?
You've vanished from view!

"Softer! Softer!" cried the 267 food-sellers. "You're hurting our ears!"

But Bashir went on singing:

Nadia, where are you?
Nadia, where are you?

When suddenly a little voice replied:

Bashir, Bashir, set me free
Or the witch will kill me!

At these words, Bashir opened his eyes and all of the 267 food-sellers leapt upon him, screeching:

"He's faking! He's faking! He can see!"

But Bashir, who was a brave boy, swung his small guitar and knocked over the nearest stallholder with a single blow. She fell flat on the ground, and the other 266 fell over all at once too, stunned just like their colleague.

Now Bashir went into all the shops on the street, one after the other, singing:

Nadia, where are you?
Nadia, where are you?

Once more, the little voice replied:

Bashir, Bashir, set me free
Or the witch will kill me!

This time there was no doubt: the voice was coming from the grocer's shop. Bashir raced inside, leaping over the vegetable display, just as, coming round from her faint, the witch-grocer opened her eyes. And, just as she came to, the other 266 food-sellers also opened their eyes. Luckily, Bashir saw her in time and, with a well-aimed blow from his guitar, he knocked them all out again for a few minutes longer.

Then, he tried to open the till, while Nadia continued to sing:

Bashir, Bashir, set me free
Or the witch will kill me!

But the drawer was too tightly closed; it wouldn't move an inch. Nadia was singing and Bashir was struggling, and all the while the 267 witch-food-sellers were waking up again. But this time, they took good care not to start opening their eyes! Instead, they kept their eyes closed and began to crawl towards the grocer's where Bashir was working away, so as to surround him.

Just then, when exhausted Bashir couldn't think which way to turn next, he saw a tall sailor go past, a well-built young man, walking down the street.

"Hello, sailor. Would you mind helping me out?"

"What can I do?"

"Could you carry this shop's till all the way to our house? My sister is stuck inside it."

"And what will my reward be?"

"You shall have the money and I'll have my sister."

"It's a deal!"

Bashir lifted the till and was just about to pass it over to the sailor when the witch-grocer, who had crept up quietly as a mouse, caught him by the foot and began to squeal:

"Ah, you thief, I have you now!"

Bashir lost his balance and dropped the till. Being very heavy indeed, when the till fell straight onto the witch-grocer's head, the single blow cracked open the heads of all 267 witch-food-sellers and knocked their brains out. This time the witch was dead, well and truly dead.

And that's not all: with the force of the impact, the till drawer flew open—*ker-CHING!* And Nadia stepped out.

She hugged and thanked her little brother, and the pair of them went home to their parents, while the sailor gathered up all the witch's blood-spattered money.

The Pair of Shoes

There once was a pair of shoes that got married. The right shoe, which was the man, was called Nicolas, and the left shoe, which was the lady, was called Tina.

They lived in a beautiful cardboard box where they lay wrapped in tissue paper. They were perfectly happy there, and they hoped things would go on like this for ever.

But then, one fine morning, a sales assistant took them out of their box so that a lady could try them on. The lady put them on, took a few steps, then, seeing that the shoes looked good on her, she said:

"I'll take them."

"Would you like the shoebox?" asked the sales assistant.

"No need," replied the lady, "I'll walk home in them."

She paid and left, her new shoes already on her feet.

So it was that Nicolas and Tina walked about for a whole day without a single glimpse of each other. Only that night were they reunited inside a dark cupboard.

"Is that you, Tina?"

"Yes, it's me, Nicolas."

"Ah, thank goodness! I thought you were lost!"

"Me too. But where were you?"

"Me? I was on the right foot."

"And I was on the left foot."

"Now I see it all," said Nicolas. "Every time you were in front, I was behind, and when you were behind, why, I was in front. That's why we couldn't see each other."

"And is this how it will be every day?" asked Tina.

"I'm afraid so!"

"But this is terrible! To spend all day without seeing you, my dear Nicolas! I shall never get used to this!"

"Listen," said Nicolas, "I have an idea. Since I am always on the right and you always on the left, well, every time I step forward, I shall make a little swerve towards you, at the same time. That way, we shall be able to say hello. All right?"

"All right!"

This, then, is what Nicolas did, in such a way that for the whole of the following day the lady wearing the shoes could not take three steps without her right foot bumping into her left heel, and every time it did—crash! She fell flat on the ground.

Very worried, that same day the lady went to consult a doctor.

"Doctor, I don't know what's wrong with me. I keep tripping myself up!"

"You trip yourself up?"

"Yes, doctor! Almost every time I take a step, my right foot catches my left heel and it makes me fall over!"

"This is very serious," said the doctor. "If it goes on, we shall have to cut off your right foot. But here is a prescription: this will get you ten thousand francs' worth of treatment. Pay me two thousand francs for the consultation, and come and see me tomorrow."

That evening, inside the cupboard, Tina asked Nicolas:

"Did you hear what the doctor said?"

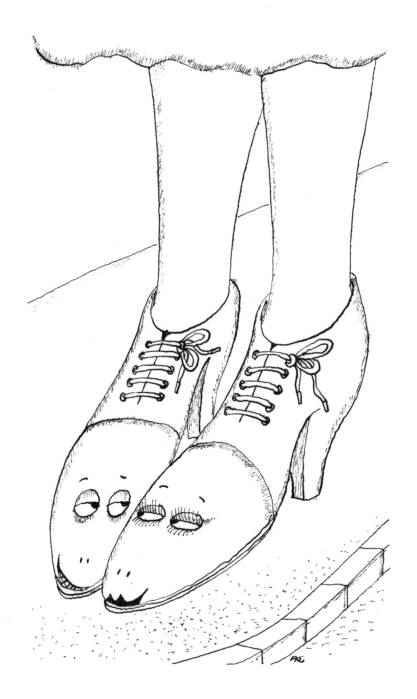

"Yes, I heard."

"This is terrible! If they cut off the lady's right foot, she will throw you out, and we will be separated for ever! We must do something!"

"Yes, but what?"

"Listen, I have an idea: since I am on the left, tomorrow, I'll be the one who makes a little swerve to the right, every time I step forward! Okay?"

"Okay!"

Tina did as she said, so that on the second day, all day long it was the left foot that bumped into the right heel, and—crash! The poor lady found herself on the ground again. Even more worried, she went back to her doctor.

"Doctor, I am going from bad to worse! Now it's my left foot that is catching on my right heel!"

"This is even more serious," said the doctor. "If this goes on, we shall have to cut off both your feet! But wait, here is a prescription: this will get you a twenty-thousand-franc treatment. Give me three thousand francs for the consultation and, above all, don't forget to come back and see me tomorrow."

That evening, Nicolas asked Tina:

"Did you hear?"

"Yes, I heard."

"If they cut off both the lady's feet, what will become of us?"

"I can't bear to think of it!"

"I still love you, Tina!"

"Me too, Nicolas, I love you!"

"I want to be with you for ever!"

"Me too, that's what I want too!"

And so they talked, in the darkness, not suspecting that the lady who had bought them was pacing up and down in the corridor, in her slippers, because she couldn't get to sleep for thinking about the doctor's diagnosis. Walking past the cupboard door, she overheard the shoes' entire conversation and, being very intelligent, she understood everything.

"So that's what it is," she thought. "It isn't me who is ill, it's my shoes who are in love! How sweet!"

Upon which, she tossed the thirty thousand francs' worth of medicines that she had bought into the rubbish bin, and the following morning told her maid:

"Do you see that pair of shoes? I shan't wear them again, but I should like to keep them all the same. Now, polish them nicely, look after them, so that they are always shiny, and above all, never separate them from each other!"

As soon as she was alone, the maid said to herself:

"Madame is mad, to keep these shoes but never wear them! In a fortnight or so, when madame has forgotten all about it, I shall steal them!"

Two weeks later, she stole them and started wearing them. But as soon as she put them on, the cleaner too began to trip herself up. One evening, while she was on the back staircase taking the rubbish out, Nicolas and Tina tried to kiss, and *badaboom! Bang! Bump!* The cleaning lady came to rest on her behind on the landing, with a bird's-nest of potato peelings on her head and a strip of apple peel dangling in a spiral between her eyes, like a lock of hair.

"These shoes are witches," she thought. "I won't try wearing them again. I'll give them to my niece; she already has a limp!"

This is what she did. The niece, who did indeed have a limp, generally spent most of her days sitting in a chair, with her feet together. When she happened to go for a walk, she walked so slowly that she could hardly get her feet caught. And the shoes were happy for, even during the day, they were mostly side by side.

This went on for a long time. Unfortunately, since the niece limped, she wore out one shoe faster than the other.

One evening, Tina said to Nicolas:

"I can feel that my sole is becoming thin, oh so thin! Very soon I shall have a hole!"

"Don't say that!" said Nicolas. "If they throw us out, we shall be separated again!"

"I know," said Tina, "but what can we do? I cannot help growing old!"

And so it happened: a week later, her sole had a hole in it. The limping niece bought a new pair of shoes and threw Nicolas and Tina into the rubbish bin.

"What will become of us?" worried Nicolas.

"I don't know," said Tina. "If only I could be sure of staying with you for ever!"

"Come close," said Nicolas, "and take my strap in yours. This way we shall not be parted."

So they did. Together they were tossed into the big bin; together they were taken away by the dustmen and left in a plot of wasteland. They stayed there together until the day when a little boy and a little girl found them.

"Oh, look at those shoes! They are arm in arm."

"That's because they're married," said the little girl.

"Well," said the little boy, "since they're married, they shall have a honeymoon!"

The little boy picked up the shoes, set them side by side on a plank, then carried the plank down to the water's edge and let it drift away, carried by the current, towards the sea. As the plank floated away, the little girl waved her handkerchief, calling:

"Goodbye, shoes, and have a wonderful journey!"

So it was that Nicolas and Tina, who were hoping for nothing more out of life, nevertheless had a beautiful honeymoon.

The Giant Who Wore Red Socks

There was once a giant who always wore bright-red socks. He was three storeys tall and lived underground.

One fine day, he said to himself:

"It's boring to stay a bachelor! Let me take a look around up there and see if I can get myself a wife."

No sooner said than done: he knocked a big hole in the ground above his head... but unfortunately, instead of popping up out among meadows, he ended up in the middle of a village.

In this village there was a young girl whose name was Mireille and who loved eating soft-boiled eggs. That particular morning, she was in fact sitting down with an egg in its egg cup, getting ready to crack it open with a teaspoon.

At the first tap of the spoon, the house began to shake.

"Gosh! Have I suddenly got stronger?" Mireille wondered.

At the second tap of the spoon, the house began to move.

"If I go on like this," she thought, "I shall bring the house right down. Perhaps it would be better if I stopped."

But since she was hungry, and she really did love soft-boiled eggs, she decided to go on all the same.

At the third tap that Mireille gave her egg, the whole house flew into the air, like a champagne cork, and, in its place, poking out of the ground, appeared the giant's head.

The young lady was herself thrown into the air. Luckily she landed in the giant's hair, so she wasn't at all hurt.

But now, running his fingers through his hair in order to shake the rubble out, the giant felt her wriggling there:

"Goodness!" he thought. "What have I got in there? Feels like some kind of creature!"

He pulled the creature out and peered at it:

"What are you?"

"I am a girl."

"What is your name?"

"Mireille."

"Mireille, I love you. I want to marry you."

"First put me down, and then I'll give my answer."

The giant put her back on the ground and Mireille ran away as fast as her legs could carry her, screaming: "Aaaaaaaaaah!"

"What did she mean by that?" wondered the giant. "That's not an answer!"

All the same, he finished pulling himself out of the ground. He was just straightening his trousers when the village mayor and vicar came along. They were both very angry.

"What on earth is this? A fine way to go about your business! Popping out of the ground like this, plumb in the middle of a residential area... Where exactly do you think you are?"

"I do apologize," replied the giant, "I didn't do it on purpose, I promise."

"And poor Mireille!" exclaimed the vicar. "Her house is quite ruined!"

"If that's all," said the giant, "then it isn't so terrible. I'll rebuild it myself!"

And there and then, he spoke the following magic words:

"By the power of my bright-red socks, let Mireille's house be set aright!"

Instantly, the house became just as it had been before, with all its walls, doors, windows and furniture, its dusty corners and even its spiderwebs! Mireille's soft-boiled egg was back in its egg cup, piping hot all over again, ready for her to eat it!

"That's better," said the vicar, calming down. "I see you're not bad at heart. Now, be on your way."

"One moment, please," said the giant. "I want to ask you something."

"What now?"

"I would like to marry Mireille."

"That's impossible," the vicar replied.

"Impossible? Why?"

"Because you are too tall. You will never fit inside the church."

"It is true that the church is very small," said the giant. "What if I blow some air inside to make it a little bigger?"

"That would be cheating," said the vicar. "The church must stay as it is. It is you who must shrink."

"I would like nothing better! How should I go about shrinking?"

There was a silence. The mayor and the vicar exchanged looks.

"Listen," said the vicar, "I like you. Let me send you to see the great Chinese wizard. While you are away, I will speak to Mireille. Come back in one year and she will be ready to marry you. But take care! She will not wait longer than a year!"

"And where does your Chinese wizard live?"

"In China."

"Thank you."

And the giant set off. It took him three months to reach China and another three months to find the wizard. He spent this time learning to speak Chinese. Standing, at last, before the wizard's house, he knocked at the door. The wizard answered the door and the giant said to him:

"Yong cho-cho-cho kong kong ngo."

Which in Chinese means: "Are *you* the great wizard?" To which the wizard replied, in a slightly different tone:

"Yong cho-cho-cho kong kong ngo."

Which means: "Yes, it's me. So?"

(Chinese is like that: you can say almost everything with a single sentence, as long as you change the intonation.)

"I would like to be shrunk," said the giant, still in Chinese.

"Fine," said the Chinese wizard, also in Chinese, "wait a minute."

He went inside, then came back with a cup full of magic potion. But the cup was too small: the giant couldn't even see it. So the wizard vanished inside again and came back with a bottle. But the bottle was too small: the giant couldn't even pick it up.

Then the wizard had an idea. He rolled his big barrel of magic potion out of the front door, then set it upright and opened it up at the top. The giant drank from the barrel just as we drink from a glass.

When he had finished drinking, he waited. Now, not only did he stay the same size but, from being bright red before, his socks turned green. The great Chinese wizard had simply given him the wrong magic potion.

Then the giant got very angry and yelled very loudly:

"Yong cho-cho-cho kong kong ngo!"

Which means: "Are you trying to make a fool of me?"

The wizard apologized and came back with another barrel, which the giant drank and his socks went red again, as they had been before.

"Now, shrink me," said the giant to the Chinese wizard, still in Chinese.

"I do apologize," said the wizard, "but I've run out of potion."

"Now what am I going to do?" cried the giant, in a desperate tone.

"Listen," said the Chinese wizard, "I like you. Let me send you to see the great Breton wizard."

"And where does your Breton wizard live?"

"In Brittany."

So the giant went on his way, saying:

"Yong cho-cho-cho kong kong ngo."

Which means "Thank you!" And the Chinese wizard watched him go, calling after him:

"Yong cho-cho-cho kong kong ngo!"

Which means: "My pleasure. *Bon voyage!*"

Three months later, the giant landed in Brittany. It took him yet another month to find the Breton wizard.

"What do you want?" asked the Breton wizard.

The giant replied:

"Yong cho-cho-cho kong kong ngo."

"Pardon?"

"Forgive me," said the giant, "I thought I was still in China. I meant to say: could you make me smaller?"

"That's very easy," said the Breton wizard.

He went into his house, then came out again with a barrel of magic potion.

"Here, drink this."

The giant drank it but, instead of shrinking, he began to grow, and was very soon twice as tall as before.

"Oh I am sorry!" said the wizard. "I must have picked up the wrong barrel of potion. Just stay there, I won't be a second."

He disappeared, and came back with another barrel.

"Here, drink this one," he said.

The giant drank and... so it proved. He shrank back to his usual height.

"This is not enough," he said. "I need to be as small as a man."

"Ah, that small? I'm sorry, that's not possible," said the wizard, "I'm all out of potion. Come back in six months."

"But I can't!" exclaimed the giant. "I must return to my fiancée within the next two months!"

And, saying this, he began to cry.

"Listen," said the wizard, "I like you, and besides, this is my fault. In view of this, I shall give you a good recommendation. Let me send you to see the Pope of Rome."

"And where does he live, this Pope of Rome?"

"In Rome."

"Thank you very much."

One month later, the giant arrived in Rome. It took him another fortnight to find the Pope's house. Once he had found it, he rang the doorbell. After a few seconds, the Pope came to the door.

"Sir... What can I do for you?"

"I want," the giant said, "to become as small as a man."

"But I am not a wizard!"

"Have pity on me, Mr Pope! My fiancée is expecting me in a fortnight!"

"What then?"

"Well, if I'm still too tall then, I won't be able to get inside the church in order to marry her!"

Hearing this, the Pope felt sorry for the giant:

"That would be sad!" he said. "Listen, my friend, I like you. I shall try to do something for you."

The Pope went into his house, picked up the telephone and dialled these three letters: HVM.

Perhaps you know, when you dial O, you are put through to the Operator. But what you may not know is that when you dial HVM, you come through to the Holy Virgin Mary. If you don't believe me, wait for a day when your parents are out, and try it!

Indeed, after a few moments, a gentle voice could be heard:

"Hello? Holy Virgin here. Who is speaking?"

"It's me, the Pope!"

"You? Ah, how lovely! And what do you want?"

"Well, it's like this: I have a giant here, who would like to become as small as a man. In order to get married, as far as I understand..."

"And does this giant of yours wear bright-red socks with special powers?"

"So he does, Holy Virgin! How did you know?"

"Well, you see, I just know!"

"Really, Holy Virgin, you are a marvel!"

"Thank you, thank you... Now, tell your giant that he should leave his red socks at the laundrette and go and soak both his feet in the sea, while calling my name. He shall see what happens next!"

"Thank you, Holy Virgin."

"That's not all! As I predict that he will still have a few problems, tell him that, afterwards, he can have three wishes, which will come true straight away. But he must be careful! Three wishes, no more!"

"I will tell him."

And the Pope repeated to the giant what the Holy Virgin Mary had told him.

Later that day, the giant handed his red socks in at the laundrette, then he went to the very edge of the sea, paddled his bare feet in the blue water, and began to call out:

"Mary! Mary! Mary!"

Pouf! He lost his footing and fell over straight away. He had become as small as a man. He swam back to shore, dried himself in the sun and went back to the laundrette.

"Good morning, madam. I've come to pick up my red socks."

"I don't have any red socks here."

"But you do! The pair of red socks, about three metres long..."

"Ah you mean: the two red sleeping bags?"

"They're socks I tell you!"

"Listen," said the laundrette assistant, "call them what you will, but when I see a sock that I can lie down in, I call it a sleeping bag!"

"Never mind, please give them back to me!"

But when he tried to put his red socks on, the poor man realized that they now came up above his head. He began to cry:

"What is to become of me? I am no longer a giant and, without my magic red socks, I'm nobody! If only they too could be shrunk down to my size!"

No sooner had he said this than his red socks shrank too, and he was able to put them on. His first wish was granted.

Very happy, he put his shoes back on and thanked the Holy Virgin, after which he thought about going back to the village where he had started out.

However, since he was no longer a giant, he could not walk all the way back to Mireille's village. Moreover, he didn't have the money to take a train. Once more he burst into tears:

"Alas! And I've only got a fortnight to get back to my fiancée! If only I could be near her!"

No sooner had he said this than he found himself in Mireille's dining room, just as the young lady herself was about to crack open a soft-boiled egg. As soon as she saw him, she jumped up and threw her arms around him:

"The vicar explained everything," she said. "I know all about what you have done for me, and now I am in love with you. In six months' time, we shall be married."

"Only in six months' time?" asked the man in red socks.

But then he had a sudden thought—that he still had his third wish to make, and so he said aloud:

"Let today be our wedding day!"

No sooner had he said this than he was stepping out of the church, in bright-red socks and a fine black suit, with Mireille at his side, all dressed in white.

From that day onwards, they lived very happily together. They have many children and the former giant, their father, earns enough for the whole family by building houses, which is easy for him, thanks to the magical powers of his bright-red socks.

Scoobidoo, the Doll
Who Could See Everything

There was once a little boy whose name was Bashir. He had a rubber doll called Scoobidoo and a papa called Sayeed.

Sayeed was a good papa, just like the good papas we all know, but Scoobidoo was no ordinary doll: she had magical powers. She walked and talked just like a person. What's more, she could see into the past and the future, and she could see things that were hidden. For her to do that, all they had to do was put a blindfold over her eyes.

She often played dominos with Bashir. When she had her eyes open, she always lost, as Bashir played better than she did. But when he blindfolded her, it was Scoobidoo who won.

One fine morning, Bashir said to his father:

"Papa, can I have a bicycle?"

"I don't have enough money," said Papa Sayeed. "Also, if I buy you a bicycle now, next year you will have grown and it will be too small. Later, in a year or two, we can think about it again."

Bashir did not mention it again, but that evening he asked Scoobidoo:

"So tell me, since you can see everything: when will I get a bicycle?"

"Blindfold me," said Scoobidoo, "and I'll tell you."

Bashir took a cloth and tied it over her eyes. Straight away Scoobidoo said:

"Yes, I do see a bicycle... But it's not for right now... It's in a year or two..."

"No sooner?"

"No sooner!"

"But I want one right now!" shouted Bashir angrily. "Look: you have magic powers, don't you?"

"I do," agreed Scoobidoo.

"Then make Papa buy me a bicycle."

"I would be happy to try, but it won't work."

"Never mind! Try anyway."

"All right: leave me blindfolded overnight, and I will try."

That night, while everyone was sleeping—Papa, Mama, Bashir and his elder sisters—Scoobidoo, in her corner, began singing very softly:

> *Papa wants a bicycle*
> *A very little bike*
> *Swift as a kite*
> *With two wheels*
> *Silent as seals*
> *With a saddle*
> *Solid as cattle*
> *With brakes*
> *Canny as snakes*
> *With a headlight*
> *Bright as a sprite*
> *And a bell*
> *Sound as a gazelle*
> *It's for Bashir*
> *Swift as a deer!*

All through the night, she sang this magical song. She stopped singing at dawn, for the magic was complete.

That morning, Papa Sayeed went to do some shopping on rue Mouffetard. To start with, he went to the baker:

"Good morning, madame."

"Good morning, Papa Sayeed. What would you like?"

"I would like a bicycle," said Papa Sayeed.

"What did you say?"

"Goodness, what am I saying? I mean: a two-pound loaf, please."

Next, Papa Sayeed went to the butcher.

"Hello, Papa Sayeed. What will it be today?"

"A good one-and-a-half pound of bike," said Papa Sayeed.

"Ah, I'm very sorry," said the butcher. "I have beef, mutton and veal, but I don't sell bicycles."

"But what nonsense am I coming out with? Of course! I meant to say: a good joint of beef, please!"

Papa Sayeed took the joint, paid and went to the grocer's next.

"Hello, Papa Sayeed. What can I get for you?"

"A pound of nice ripe bicycles," said Papa Sayeed.

"A pound of what?" asked the grocer.

"What is wrong with me, today? A pound of ripe white grapes, please!"

This is how it was, all day. Every time Papa Sayeed went into a shop, he began by asking for some bicycle. Just like that, without meaning to; he couldn't help it. So it happened that he asked for another box of white bicycles in the grocer's, a good slice of bicycle at the cheese shop, and a bottle of bicycle bleach at the laundrette. Finally, very worried, he dropped in to see his doctor.

"Hullo there, Papa Sayeed, what is the problem?"

"Well, it's like this," said Papa Sayeed. "Since this morning, I don't know what's wrong with me but, each time I go into a shop, I start by asking for a bicycle. It's against my will, I assure you, I'm not doing it on purpose in the least! What is this sickness? I'm very disturbed by it... Couldn't you give me a little bicycle... There you are! It's happening again! I mean a little medicine, to stop it happening?"

"Ahem," said the doctor. "Curious, very curious indeed... Tell me, Papa Sayeed, you wouldn't happen to have a young son, by any chance?"

"Yes, I do, doctor."

"And this young son has recently asked you for a bicycle..."

"How do you know that?"

"Heh heh! It's my job! And your son would not happen to have a doll, by any chance? A rubber doll known as Scoobidoo?"

"He does indeed, doctor!"

"So I thought! Well then, watch out for that doll, Papa Sayeed. If she is to stay with you, she will make you buy a bicycle, whether you like it or not. And—that will be three thousand francs!"

"Oh no! They're much more expensive than that!"

"I'm not talking about a bicycle, I'm talking about your medical consultation. You owe me three thousand francs."

"Yes, of course!"

Papa Sayeed paid the doctor, went back home and said to little Bashir:

"Would you do me a favour and get rid of your doll, because if I find her I shall throw her in the fire!"

As soon as Bashir and Scoobidoo were alone:

"You see," said Scoobidoo, "I did tell you that it wouldn't work... But don't be sad. I will go away and

I'll come back in a year's time. On my return, you shall have your bicycle. However, there's something I will need before I go..."

"What's that?" asked Bashir.

"Well, when I'm alone, you will no longer be there to blindfold me... So I would like you to make me a pair of glasses with wooden lenses."

"But I don't know how to do that!"

"Ask your Papa."

Only too happy to know the doll was leaving, Papa Sayeed agreed to make her a pair of glasses with wooden lenses. He cut the lenses out of a piece of plywood with a little saw, made a frame out of wire, and said to Scoobidoo:

"How do you like these?"

Scoobidoo tried on the glasses. They suited her straight away.

"Very nice, sir, thank you very much."

"Okay. Now, out you go!" said Papa Sayeed.

"Of course. Goodbye, sir. Goodbye, Bashir."

And Scoobidoo left.

She journeyed for a long, long time, walking by night and hiding by day, in order not to attract attention. After three weeks, she came to a great

port on the shore of the English Channel. It was night-time. A large ship was at the dock, ready to depart early the following morning and begin its long journey around the world.

Putting on her glasses, Scoobidoo thought to herself:

"This ship is just right for me."

She put her glasses back in her pocket, then stationed herself at the foot of the gangway, and there she waited.

On the stroke of three in the morning, a sailor walking in zigzags rolled up to the gangway and was about to step onto it when he heard a tiny voice calling to him from ground level:

"Mister sailor! Mister sailor!"

"Who's there?" asked the sailor.

"Me, Scoobidoo! I'm right in front of you. Look out, you're about to step on me!"

The sailor crouched down:

"Well I never! How strange. A talking doll! And what might you be after?"

"I want you to take me onto the ship with you."

"And how will you make yourself useful?"

"I can see into the future and predict the weather."

"Really! Then, tell me what the weather will be tomorrow morning."

"Just a moment, please."

Scoobidoo took out her glasses, put them on, then said without hesitation:

"Tomorrow morning the weather will be bad. So bad that you won't be able to leave the port."

The sailor burst out laughing.

"Ha ha ha! You know nothing about it! We'll have fine weather, as it happens, and we weigh anchor at dawn."

"And I say you won't be able to leave!"

"All right then, let's bet on it, if you like? If the weather is good enough for us to go, I will leave you behind. But if bad weather holds us back, I'll take you along. Is it a deal?"

"It's a deal."

And so it happened that, the following day, the sun had hardly risen when a great cloud appeared in the north-west and spread so, so quickly that within five minutes the whole sky had turned black. Then the storm broke, so wild and violent that the ship was obliged to stay where she was.

"I don't understand at all," said the captain. "The forecast said it would be fine!"

"Well," said the sailor, "I know a doll that predicted this bad weather."

"A doll? You'd had a few drinks, hadn't you?"

"I'd drunk a good many," said the sailor, "but even so. She's a little rubber doll called Scoobidoo."

"And where is this Scoobidoo?"

"There, on the dock; I can see her from here."

"Bring her here."

The sailor leant over the rail and called:

"Here, Scoobidoo! Come up, will you? The captain would like to talk to you."

As soon as Scoobidoo was on board, the captain asked her:

"What is it that you can do, exactly?"

And Scoobidoo replied:

"I can see into the past and the future, and I can see things that are hidden."

"Is that all you can do? All right, tell me something about my family!"

"Right away, captain!"

Putting on her glasses, Scoobidoo began to speak very quickly, as if she were reading from a book:

"You have a wife in Le Havre, with a blond child. You have a wife in Singapore, with two yellow children. You have a wife in Dakar, with six black children..."

"Enough, enough!" exclaimed the captain. "You can come with me. Don't say another word!"

"And how much will you pay me?" asked Scoobidoo.

"Well, how much do you want?"

"I would like five new francs per day, to buy a bicycle for Bashir."

"Done. You'll be paid on your return."

So it was that Scoobidoo set off to sail around the world. The captain tied her to the bulkhead in his cabin with a pink ribbon, and every morning he asked her:

"Will it be rain or shine today?"

Thanks to her glasses, Scoobidoo replied correctly every time.

The great ship sailed right around Spain, on past Italy, past Egypt, through the Indian Ocean, past Thailand, through the Pacific Ocean, crossed into the Atlantic via the Panama Canal, then headed back towards Europe.

*

One fine morning, when the ship was nearing the coast of France, the cook snuck into the captain's cabin. Scoobidoo enquired:

"What are you doing in here?"

"Have a guess," replied the cook.

Scoobidoo took out her glasses, put them on and gasped:

"You've come to steal my glasses!"

"Right you are," said the cook.

And, before Scoobidoo had time to think, he snatched them from her, slipped back out of the cabin and threw them into the sea.

A few minutes later, as if on cue, the captain came back into the cabin.

"So tell me, Scoobidoo, what weather shall we have tomorrow morning?"

"I can't say," replied the doll, "the cook has stolen my glasses."

The captain raised an eyebrow: "Glasses or no glasses, you promised to forecast the weather. What do you think? That I'll keep on paying you for nothing?"

The captain was pretending to be angry, but in fact it was he who had sent the cook to steal the glasses, because he did not want to pay Scoobidoo what he owed her.

"You may get along however you like," he said, "but if you don't tell me what weather we'll have tomorrow morning, I shall throw you into the sea!"

"All right... let's say: it will be sunny!" said Scoobidoo, making a guess.

Alas! As early as sunrise the next day, a fat black cloud appeared on the horizon and began to spread rapidly, as if it was trying to gobble up the sky. At the same time, a storm was setting in and the ship began to pitch from side to side. The captain came in—or pretended to come in—in a terrible fury.

"You have deceived me!" he thundered at Scoobidoo.

And then, paying no attention to her protests, he threw her overboard.

Poor, dazed Scoobidoo saw the sea and the sky spin around her before she dropped into the water. Almost immediately, a great mouth full of pointed teeth opened wide beneath her, and she was swallowed up by a shark that had been following the ship for several days.

Since the shark was very greedy, it swallowed her without chewing, so that Scoobidoo found herself in its stomach, not too comfortable, but not the least bit

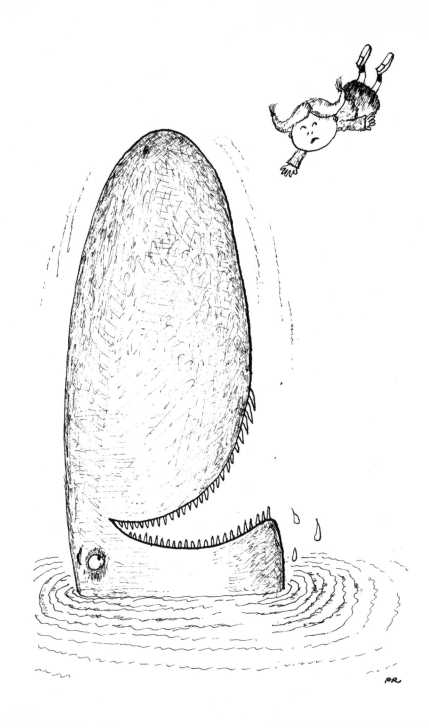

hurt. She tried to feel her way about in the dark, all the while muttering to herself:

"What will become of me here? And what about my poor little Bashir, still waiting for his bicycle?"

So it was that, talking aloud in the pitch darkness, Scoobidoo came across something that felt like a miniature bicycle: it had two round blocks of wood, linked together by a wire frame.

"Well I never... my glasses!"

They were indeed her glasses, which the shark had swallowed the day before. Scoobidoo picked them up, put them on and straight away saw everything as clear as day, there inside the stomach of the great fish. She exclaimed happily:

"And there's treasure in here!"

Upon which, without the least hesitation, she turned towards a fat oyster that was lying, wide open, in a fold in the shark's stomach.

"Hello, oyster!"

"Hello, doll!"

"Am I right in thinking you have a big pearl inside you there?"

"Alas, you are quite right!" replied the oyster, sighing. "A very big pearl, which is hurting me horribly! If only I could find someone to take this lump of dirt away!"

"Would you like me to take it?"

"Now, if you were to do that, you would be doing me a great service!"

"Open yourself up very wide, then, and we shall see!"

The oyster opened up as wide as she could. Scoobidoo plunged both hands in and plucked out the pearl.

"Ooowww!" exclaimed the oyster.

"There, there, now, it's all over."

And Scoobidoo held up the pearl. It was enormous, a magnificent pearl. It was worth enough money to buy five or six bicycles! Scoobidoo put it into her pocket and said politely to the oyster:

"Thank you."

"Not at all—thank *you*! If I can do anything for you..."

"You might be able to give me some advice," said Scoobidoo.

"Of course!"

"What should I do to make my way home?"

"It's very simple," said the oyster. "Since you have two legs, you have only to hop from one foot to the other. That will make the shark feel sick, and he will do anything you ask."

"Thank you, kind oyster!"

And Scoobidoo began hopping from one foot to the other.

After a minute, the shark began to feel unwell. After two minutes, he had hiccups. After three minutes, he was seasick. After five minutes, he called out:

"Hey, are you quite finished in there? Can't you sit quietly and let me digest you?"

"Take me to Paris!" Scoobidoo called to him.

"To Paris? Whatever next? I do not take orders from my food!"

"In that case, I'll keep hopping!"

"No, no! Stop! Where is it, this Paris?"

"You get there by swimming up the River Seine."

"Err—what? Swim up the River Seine? But I shall be a laughing stock! I am a fish of the open ocean! No one in my family has ever left salt water!"

"Then I'll keep on hopping!"

"No, no! Have pity! I'll go wherever you wish. But do stay still a bit!"

And the great fish set off. He swam as far as the port of Le Havre, then he swam up the River Seine, through Rouen and all the way to Paris. Once there, he stopped beside a stone staircase at the water's edge, opened his mouth and called out as loudly as he could:

"End of the line; all change please! All change! Out you get, now, scarper. I hope I never see you again!"

Scoobidoo got out and climbed up onto the riverbank. It was about three o'clock in the morning. No one was in the streets, nor was there even one star in the sky. Taking advantage of the darkness and with the help of her glasses, the doll quickly made her way back to rue Broca. The following morning, she knocked on Papa Sayeed's door and handed him the pearl. Papa Sayeed thanked her, then took the pearl to the jeweller, and was at last able to buy a bicycle for Bashir.

As for the ship on which Scoobidoo had sailed away, it was never seen again. I do believe it came to a watery end.

The Story of Lustucru

That day, in the classroom, the teacher asked the children the following question:

"What is the name of the Roman general who conquered the land of Gaul?"

Little Bashir raised his hand for permission to speak and said:

"Lustucru."

The teacher did not look pleased.

But when Monsieur Pierre heard this story, he asked straight away:

"But what if Bashir was right? The truth, as they say, comes from the mouths of babes and infants... There's nothing for it: I must look this up!"

And Monsieur Pierre looked it up thoroughly. He

reread all the great writers: the Brothers Grimm, Hans Andersen and all the rest; he paced up and down, he thought long and hard; he sat down and lay down; he slept and he dreamt—and after a week of hard work, he was ready to tell the story of Lustucru.

This is the tale he told:

A very long time ago, in ancient-Roman times, there lived a barbarian king. When this king had a son, a good fairy appeared and said the following words to him:

"Your son is immortal; he will never die. What's more, he will grow up into a great warrior, full of courage and audacity, and he will accomplish great things. But all this on one condition!"

"What's that?" asked the King.

"It is," the fairy said, "that you call him Lustucru."

The King hesitated. Lustucru is a rather silly name, even for a fierce barbarian. Then he reasoned to himself that it would be worth bearing this small inconvenience for the sake of courage and immortality and all the rest of it, and so, having thought it all through, he replied:

"I accept."

"Then let it be so," said the fairy.

And she disappeared.

Prince Lustucru grew up quickly and soon he was a magnificent boy, full of strength and courage. When he was about twelve years old, his father the King sent him to Rome to complete his education.

There he joined a Roman school. Being as clever as he was courageous, he came top in everything. Or rather, he ought to have come top, but his Roman teachers never put him in first place because nothing in the world could make them agree to say or write: top of the class, Lustucru.

Throughout his schooling, then, poor Lustucru remained forever in second place. On leaving school, he tried to join the Civil Service and indeed he passed all the exams. However, the same curse followed him here too. Even though he was by far the most brilliant and able applicant, he was never accepted, and all his rivals pipped him, as they say, to the post.

What could he do? In his place, a lesser boy would

have left Rome and gone back home to his parents. But Lustucru knew he was better than that; he was sure he had been born to do great things. He thought to himself:

"I am better than all the others, but that is not enough. For my talent to be recognized, I shall have to do something huge! But what? Let's see, let's see... I've got it! A brilliant idea! I shall conquer Gaul!"

Just to remind you: back then, France was known as "Gaul" and the French people were called the Gauls.

Now, Gaul was a very big piece of land and Lustucru would not be able to conquer it by himself. He needed to recruit an army.

One day, while he was walking in the streets of Rome, a beggar stopped him.

"Have pity, sir, give me something!"

Lustucru looked at the beggar. He was poor and dirty but he was a handsome man for all that, still young, well built, brave and willing.

"Tell me: do you know how to fight?"

"Oh yes, sir!"

"Do you like travelling?"

"Oh yes!"

"You're not afraid of adventures?"

"Oh no!"

"In that case," said Lustucru, "you shall join my service. You are to raise an army for me, and we are going to conquer Gaul. Okay?"

"Okay!" said the beggar.

"Very good! Incidentally, what is your name?"

"Julius Caesar."

"Right then, Julius Caesar, follow me. I'll buy you some lunch."

So Julius Caesar became Lustucru's second-in-command. Between the two of them, they raised an army, trained it and drilled it, and then they crossed the Alps from Italy and marched into the land of Gaul.

Everyone knows the story of their victory. As the Gaulish tribes could not stop fighting amongst themselves, Lustucru began by making alliances with some tribes and playing them off against the others. In this way, he reached the heart of the land. Then he helped the Gauls in their battles against the Germans, which allowed him to work his way even further into favour. But, little by little, the Gauls began to notice that, instead of helping them,

Lustucru was actually taking over Gaul. At this, they resolved to forget their quarrels and come together once and for all to drive the Romans out. The young king of the Arvernes tribe, a certain Vercingetorix, took charge of the movement, and this time it was open war. By rights, the Romans ought to have been wiped out, for they were only a handful of men in the middle of a hostile country. But while they were courageous and energetic, the Gauls were terribly lacking in discipline and team spirit. In the end, having retreated to the town of Alesia, Vercingetorix was forced to admit defeat and gave himself up to Lustucru.

Lustucru wrote the whole story down in a book and gave it to Julius Caesar, saying:

"Take this book to the Romans, and bring Vercingetorix along to show them too. Tell them that Lustucru has conquered the land of Gaul for them."

But Julius Caesar was both envious and jealous. He took a rubber, a reed pen and some ink, and he rewrote the story. Everywhere the name *Lustucru* appeared, he rubbed it out and wrote *Caesar*; everywhere he found *Lustucrum*, he put *Caesarem*; and everywhere he found *Lustucro*, he replaced it with *Caesari* or

Caesare. In short, wherever Lustucru's name appeared, he rubbed it out and put his own.

When Caesar got to Rome, he told the Roman senators:

"I, Julius Caesar, have just conquered Gaul. Here is the book in which I tell of my adventures. And now, you must make me emperor."

"Oh, is that what you think?" replied the Romans.

"If you won't do it," retorted Julius Caesar, "I'll send my army to fight you!"

"Oh, well, in that case..." said the Romans.

And they crowned him Emperor of Rome.

Caesar entered Rome in the midst of a superb parade and immediately had Vercingetorix strangled, so he could not tell the truth about Gaul. Then Caesar sent two of his men back to Gaul, with orders to kill Lustucru. As soon as they arrived, Lustucru, who had been waiting impatiently for news from Rome, had them brought to his tent. Inside the tent, the two men drew their swords and ran his heart through. Although he was immortal, Lustucru was still painfully surprised. He realized that once again he had been robbed of first place and, sickened and frustrated, he retreated to Germania.

The Germans allowed him to live among them because of his bravery, but they refused to let him lead them. They didn't want to take orders from a gentleman called Lustucru any more than the Romans did. Once more, our hero had to settle for an inferior position.

A few centuries later, the Germans invaded the Roman Empire and the Franks occupied Gaul. Have you heard of Clovis, king of the Franks? Well, at that time, Lustucru was one of Clovis's warriors.

In the year 486, after defeating the last of the Roman armies still stationed in Gaul, Clovis seized the town of Soissons and ransacked it. All the valuable things found there were gathered together and then given away in a raffle. Lustucru won a fabulous vase from the church of Soissons. When the raffle was over, King Clovis came to make Lustucru an offer:

"Give me your vase," he said, "and I'll give you something in exchange..."

But, fed up of being treated like a nobody, Lustucru flew into a rage. With one swing of his axe, he smashed the precious vase into smithereens, saying to Clovis:

"You'll have only your share, nothing more!"

Clovis left without another word. But, since he

tended to bear grudges, he did not forget this scene. A few weeks later, coming across his soldier Lustucru, Clovis dropped his weapons on the ground. Lustucru bent down to pick them up. As he did so, Clovis brandished *his* battleaxe and split Lustucru's head in two, saying:

"This is no more than you did with the vase from Soissons!"

And off he went, believing he had killed Lustucru. In fact, Lustucru only went to bed with a serious migraine, but he also left Clovis's army for good.

At that point, we lose track of him for quite a while. Besides, it would be impossible for us to tell you every detail of his long, long life, even if we had all the necessary records.

In the year 732, the Arabs came up from Spain and occupied the South of France. Hoping to stop their advance, the Frankish leader, Charles Martel, took the Frankish army to meet them. The two armies fought the Battle of Poitiers. It was very bloody and went on all day long. When night fell, the two armies withdrew to their camps, although nobody knew exactly who had won. Everyone was very tired, and the two sides went to sleep.

Lustucru, however, stayed awake. He crept unseen out of the Frankish camp and attacked the Arab camp, all by himself. In less than an hour, he had killed hundreds of the enemy. However hard the poor Muslims defended themselves, whether with swords, lances, axes or maces, Lustucru went on slaughtering them, and his wounds went on vanishing as soon as they were made. Seeing this, the Arabs took him for the Devil, struck their camp and scarpered without waiting for dawn.

The following morning, Charles Martel woke up and saw that the enemy had retreated.

"Look at this! How peculiar!" he said. "So who drove them away?"

"I did!" said a soldier, saluting him.

"You did? What is your name?"

"My name is Lustucru!"

Hearing his name, the entire Frankish army burst out laughing, and Charles Martel giggled:

"That's ridiculous! How will we sound if we go about saying that Lustucru beat the Arabs at Poitiers? Let it be thoroughly understood that they were beaten by me. And whoever says they weren't shall have his head cut off!"

So it was that, once again, the name of Lustucru was rubbed out of history.

Lustucru went on to do many more things. It was he who sounded the horn at Roncevaux, in the year 778. It was he who conquered England for the Normans in 1066. It was he too who drove the English out of France: Du Guesclin, the Eagle of Brittany, was in fact Lustucru; the Great Ferré was Lustucru too; Joan of Arc was also Lustucru... It was Lustucru who recognized Louis XVI at Varennes and who composed the French national anthem, the Marseillaise. It was not Napoleon who crossed the Bridge of Arcole on foot beneath a hail of Austrian bullets—no, it was Lustucru, Lustucru every time! Some might even claim that it was he who, on the 18th June 1940, at the microphone of Radio London, made a certain wartime broadcast... but we must stop there. Go any further and we'll get mixed up in politics.

Poor Lustucru had lived a good two thousand years by this time, and despite all his astounding feats, his name remained unknown to history. Thoroughly discouraged, he went to find the great witch of rue Mouffetard.

"Good morning, Madame Witch."

"Good morning, monsieur. You're looking rather sad. What on earth is wrong?"

"Well, it's this: I am tall, I am strong, I am brave and I'm immortal. I've done hundreds of great things that everyone knows about, but nobody knows that I'm the one who did them, and nobody knows my name!"

"That is a strange case," said the witch. "And what is your name?"

"My name is Lustucru."

"Lustucru? Now I understand! My poor monsieur, with a name like that, historians will *never* give you any of the credit!"

"Do you really think so?"

"I'm sure of it! If you want to be famous, there's only one thing to do..."

"What's that?"

"Have a song written about you!"

"That's a great idea! But how?"

"I haven't a clue," said the witch. "And it looks as though nobody else does either. Why people like Malbrough and King Dagobert are praised in popular songs while the Great Condé and King Chilperic aren't is a mystery to me. All you can do is wait. After all, there's no rush: you are immortal already!"

"That's true," said Lustucru.

He thanked the witch, then left Paris and, resigned to a long life of mediocrity, he settled down in a small village where he bought a beautiful house on the high street.

Months went by, then years. Every morning, Lustucru sat in a big armchair by his open window and spent the day gazing over at his neighbour opposite, a certain Madame Michel, who lived alone in a house with green shutters and only her cat for company. Looking at Madame Michel like that, every day, he ended up falling in love with her. One fine Sunday after church, he bought a bunch of flowers, smoothed out his best Sunday suit and put on his tie and gloves, then he crossed the road and rang his neighbour's doorbell. She opened the door.

"Monsieur... What can I do for you?"

"Forgive me, Madame Michel, I am your neighbour from across the road..."

"You're my neighbour? I hardly recognized you! How handsome you are! Do come in for five minutes. Won't you have a little something with me?"

"With pleasure, Madame Michel... Here: some flowers for you!"

"Oh, you are kind! And they *are* pretty! Do sit down; I'll put them in some water."

"Tell me, Madame Michel..."

"I'm all ears, neighbour."

"In that case... I have come to ask for your hand in marriage."

"You want to marry me?"

"Yes, Madame Michel."

"Oh, but that's impossible! I hardly know you..."

"You will come to know me, Madame Michel. You can see already that I am tall, I am strong, I am brave and, what's more, I am immortal!"

"Goodness me," she said, "I must admit I'm interested. And what is your name?"

"My name is Lustucru."

As soon as she heard this name, Madame Michel's face fell; horrified, she replied:

"Oh no, neighbour, this cannot be! You are a fine man, I won't deny it, you are even very pleasant, but I am a serious woman. I have no desire to be the laughing stock of the whole county! Ask me anything, but not to call myself Madame Lustucru. I would much rather remain alone!"

Once more, poor Lustucru's plans were foiled by his own name. But this time he was in love, and he would not admit defeat.

That evening, while standing at the door of his house enjoying the fresh air, Lustucru caught sight of a dim shadow slinking along by the side of the road. Looking more carefully, he recognized his neighbour's cat. He called:

"Pussy! Pussy!"

Unafraid, the cat came over, wanting to be stroked. Lustucru snatched him up, carried him into the house and then locked him in a small shed, right at the bottom of his garden. After which he went to bed, chuckling to himself and rubbing his hands.

The following morning, on the stroke of eight, Lustucru was violently awoken by high-pitched shrieks. It was Madame Michel, at her window, wailing:

"Alas, my little pussycat! Where is my little pussycat? I've lost him! Has nobody seen my little pussy? Who will bring back my little pussycat?"

Lustucru got up and popped his head out of the window.

"Hello there, Madame Michel, what's wrong?"

"Ah, Monsieur Lustucru, it's my little pussycat! I've lost my little pussy!"

"Why, not at all, you haven't lost him."

"What do you mean? Do you know where he is?"

"I do indeed."

"Where is he?"

"With me."

"With you? Oh, thank goodness! I'll come and pick him up right away."

"Just a moment, Madame Michel. I did not say I would give him back to you!"

"What—you won't give him back? But you have no right! He is my little pussycat! I cannot live without my little pussy!"

"And I, Madame Michel, I cannot live without you! Marry me, and I will give back your cat."

"And if I refuse?"

"If you refuse, I will eat him!"

"Oh, this is too much! I shall call the police!"

"As you wish! Off you go and call the police, and while you're busy, I'll just be putting the cat on the stove to stew."

At these words, Madame Michel began to weep:

"Oh, Monsieur Lustucru! Why are you so wicked?"

"Because I love you, Madame Michel!"

Madame Michel stared at him in amazement:

"Do you love me as much as that?"

"I do, Madame Michel!"

This time, Madame Michel was quite moved.

"Poor man!" she thought. "I didn't know there were still men capable of such great love! After all, Lustucru isn't such a terrible name... One would grow used to it, in the end..."

And aloud she said:

"If I marry you, will you give back my cat?"

"I will give him back."

"You won't do him any harm?"

"I will do him no harm at all."

"Cross your heart and hope to die?"

"Cross my heart and hope to die."

"All right, I accept. I will marry you."

"Really, truly?"

"Really, truly!"

"For ever and ever?"

"For ever and ever!"

"Cross your heart and hope to die?"

"Cross my heart and hope to die!"

"Oh, what joy! Thank you Madame Michel!"

Lustucru dressed and came downstairs and, without further delay, returned his neighbour's cat. Six months later they were married and, just as the newly wedded couple were leaving the church, the local children began to sing:

Here's Missis Michel who lost her cat
Who calls from her window for it to come back.
Here's old Lustucru
Who'll return her halloo—
Missis, now you've your cat and a lover anew!

"What's this song you're singing?" Lustucru asked them.

"It's a brand-new song that we're singing about you," the children answered.

"I think it's a stupid song," said Madame Michel.

"Well," said Lustucru, "I think it's fantastic!"

Since that day, old Lustucru has lived in perfect happiness in his small village, with his wife and her cat. Every time the local children come across him, they sing his song so as to please him, and he gives them money to buy sweets.

The Fairy in the Tap

There was once a fairy, a sweet little fairy who lived in a freshwater spring, not far from a village. You know, don't you, that in the old days, the land of Gaul was not Christian, and that our ancestors the Gauls used to worship fairies. In those times, the villagers worshipped this little fairy. They decorated her spring with flowers, brought her cakes and fruit and, on holy days, they even put on their finest clothes and there went to dance for her.

Then, one day, Gaul became a Christian land and the vicar banned the local people from bringing offerings and going to dance around the spring. He claimed that they would lose their souls and that the fairy was a demon. The villagers were quite sure this wasn't true; still, they didn't dare contradict the vicar, because they were afraid of him. But the oldest villagers continued to go in secret and leave their gifts beside the spring. When the vicar realized this, he was very cross. He had a great stone crucifix set up beside the spring, then he organized a procession and pronounced a whole string of magic words over the spring, in Latin, in order to drive the fairy away. And the people really believed he had managed to chase her away, for no more was heard of her for the next 1,500 years. The older people who had worshipped her died; little by little, the young people forgot about her, and their grandchildren never even knew that she had existed. Even the vicars, her sworn enemies, stopped believing in her.

Yet, the fairy had not abandoned her spring. She was still there, deep in the spring, but she was hiding, for the crucifix stopped her from coming out. Besides, she had understood that nobody cared about her any longer.

"Patience!" she advised herself. "Our time is past, but the Christians' time will also pass. One day, that crucifix will crumble away, and I shall be free once more..."

One day, two men came walking up by the spring. They were engineers. They noticed that the water was plentiful and clear, and decided to use it to supply fresh water to the nearby town.

A few weeks later, the labourers arrived. They pulled down the crucifix, which was in their way, then they enclosed the spring and channelled its water in pipes, all the way to the town.

This is how, one fine day, the fairy discovered she was living in a network of pipes, whose twists and turns she began to follow blindly for miles, wondering all the while what on earth had happened to her spring. The farther she went, the narrower the pipes became, branching off into even more, secondary pipes. The fairy turned and turned again, now to the left, now to the right, and in the end she popped out of a great copper tap, over a big sink made of stone.

She was lucky, really, for she could just as easily have come out in a toilet cistern, and then, instead of being the fairy in the tap, she would have become the fairy in the toilet. Thank goodness that didn't happen.

The tap and the sink were part of a kitchen, and the kitchen happened to be part of a house where a family of working people lived: a father, a mother and their two teenage daughters. It was some time before they saw the fairy, for fairies do not come out during the day, only after midnight. It so happened that the father was a hard worker, so was the mother, and the two daughters went to school, so everybody was in bed by ten in the evening at the latest, and nobody ever turned on the tap during the night.

One night, however, the elder daughter—who was greedy and not very well behaved—got up at two in the morning, to go and see what she could find in the fridge. She found a roast chicken thigh, had a nibble at that, ate a mandarin, dipped her finger into a pot of jam and licked it; then she felt thirsty. She took a glass out of the dresser, went to the tap, turned it on... when suddenly, instead of water, out of the tap flew a tiny lady in a purple dress, fluttering dragonfly wings and clutching a wand topped with a golden star in her hand. The fairy (for it was she) perched on the edge of the sink and said in a musical voice:

"Hello, Martine."

(I forgot to tell you that the girl's name was Martine.)

"Hello madame," replied Martine.

"Would you do something for me, Martine?" asked the good fairy. "Would you give me a little jam, please?"

As I said, Martine was a bit greedy and not at all well behaved. Nevertheless, when she saw that the fairy was nicely dressed and had dragonfly wings and a magic wand, she said to herself:

"Look out! She is a fine lady and I must be careful to be polite to her!"

So she replied, with a hypocritical smile:

"But of course, madame! Right away, madame!"

She took a clean spoon, dug it into the jam jar and held it out to the good fairy. The fairy fluttered her wings and hovered around the spoon, taking a few quick licks with her tongue, then she settled on the sideboard and said:

"Thank you, Martine. In recognition of your kindness, I shall give you a gift: for every word you say, a pearl shall fall from your mouth."

And the fairy disappeared.

"Fancy that!" exclaimed Martine.

And, as she said these words, two pearls fell from her mouth.

The following morning, she told her parents the whole story, while spitting out a fair number of pearls.

Her mother took these pearls to the jeweller, who

pronounced them of very good quality, although a little small.

"If she said some longer words," suggested the father, "they might come out bigger..."

They asked their neighbours to tell them the longest word they knew. A well-read neighbour came up with the word *antidisestablishmentarianism*. They made Martine say it several times. She obeyed, but the pearls were no bigger. A little more elongated, perhaps, and a little more irregular in shape. What's more, as it is a very difficult word, Martine could not say it well, and the quality of her pearls began to suffer.

"Never mind," said her parents. "In any case, our fortune is made. From today, our daughter will no longer go to school. She will stay here at the table, and she will talk all day over the salad bowl. And if she dare stop talking, she'll be for it!"

Being, among other faults, lazy and a chatterbox, Martine was delighted with this plan at first. But after two days, she had had enough of sitting still and talking in an empty room. After three days it was misery, and after four it was pure torture. On the evening of the fifth day, at dinnertime, she came inside, in a towering rage, and began to scream:

"Drat! Drat! Drat!"

Actually, she didn't say *drat* but something much worse. And with these three bad words, three great pearls appeared, enormous baubles, rolling down onto the tablecloth.

"What on earth?..." her parents chorused.

But they understood straight away.

"It's simple," said Martine's father, "I should have thought of it. Every time she says an ordinary word, she coughs up a small pearl. But when it's a naughty word, out comes a big one."

From that day, Martine's parents made her pronounce nothing but swear words over the salad bowl. At first, this made her feel better, but soon her parents were telling her off every time she said anything that wasn't a swear word. After a week, her life had come to feel unbearable, and she ran away from home.

Martine walked the streets of Paris all day long, not knowing where to go. Towards evening, starving hungry and quite exhausted, she sat down on a bench. Seeing her there alone, a young man came and sat beside her. He had wavy hair, white hands and a very charming look to him. He spoke to her very kindly, and so she told him her story. He listened with great interest, all the while collecting in his cap the pearls she dropped while confiding in him. When she had finished, he looked tenderly into her eyes:

"Go on talking," he said. "You are magnificent. If only you knew how I love hearing you speak! Let's stay together, shall we? You can sleep in my room and we shall never leave each others' sides. We shall be happy!"

Not knowing where else she could go, Martine accepted willingly. The young man took her home to his house, gave her food and a place to sleep, and the following morning, when she woke up, he told her:

"Now, my dear, it's time to discuss serious matters. I can't be feeding you to do nothing. I have to go out, so I'm locking you in. This evening, when I get back, I would like our big soup tureen to be full of big pearls—and if it is not full, you shall hear about it!"

All that day and all of those that followed, Martine was stuck indoors and obliged to fill the soup tureen with pearls. The young man with his kind eyes locked her in every morning and only came back in the evening. And if, when he came back, the tureen was not full, he beat Martine.

But let us leave Martine and her sad fate for a moment, and return to her parents' house.

Martine's younger sister, who was sensible and well behaved, had been deeply affected by the whole story, and had not the slightest wish to meet the fairy in the tap. Nevertheless, her parents, who bitterly regretted their eldest daughter's disappearance, would say every evening:

"You know, if you're thirsty in the night, you're quite free to go and get a glass of water in the kitchen..."

Or:

"Now you're a big girl. You could perfectly well do something nice for your parents. After all we have done for you..."

But Marie (I forgot to tell you that her name was Marie) pretended she had no idea what they meant.

One day, her mother had a brainwave. For dinner she served: split-pea soup, herring fillets and salt pork with lentils, and goats' cheese for afters, which was all so salty that, when she went to bed, Marie could not sleep for thirst. For two hours she lay awake in bed, saying to herself:

"I won't go to the kitchen. I won't go to the kitchen..."

But in the end, she went, still hoping that the fairy would not come out.

Alas! Hardly had she turned the tap when out popped the fairy and fluttered down to perch on Marie's shoulder.

"Marie, you're such a good girl, give me a little jam!"

Marie was a very good girl, but she wasn't stupid, so she answered:

"No thanks! I don't need your gifts. You have made my sister miserable—that's quite enough for me! Besides, I'm not allowed to go looking in the fridge while my parents are in bed."

Out of touch with people for the last 1,500 years and no longer used to ordinary conversation, the fairy was offended by Marie's reply. In her disappointment, she snapped:

"Since you are so unpleasant, my gift to you is that, with every word you say, a snake will fall from your mouth!"

*

101

Indeed, the very next day, with the first word Marie spoke to try to tell her parents about the fairy, she spat out a grass snake. She had to give up on speaking and instead wrote down what had happened during the night.

In a state of panic, Marie's parents took her to see a doctor who lived two floors up in the same building. The doctor was young, friendly, well regarded in the neighbourhood and showed great promise in his career. He listened to the parents' story, then he gave Marie his most delightful smile and said:

"Now, there's no need to worry. It may not be all that serious. Would you like to follow me into my bathroom?"

They all went into the bathroom. There, the doctor said to Marie:

"Lean over the bathtub. Like that. And now, say a word. Any word."

"Mummy," said Marie.

And a long grass snake slithered from her mouth into the bath.

"Very good," said the doctor. "And now, say a swear word, just to see..."

Marie blushed all over.

"Come on," said her mother, "just one naughty word for the doctor!"

Shyly, Marie muttered a swear word. And a young boa constrictor uncoiled into the bath.

"How sweet she is!" exclaimed the doctor, touched. "Now, my dear Marie, make one more effort and say something really mean for me."

Marie realized that she had to obey. But she was so good that, even if she didn't mean it, merely saying something nasty was hard for her. Still, she forced herself, and in a low voice pronounced:

"Dirty cow."

Right away, two little adders rolled up in balls, flew from her mouth and fell with two soft thuds on top of the other snakes.

"It's exactly as I thought," said the doctor, gratified. "For a swear word, we get a big snake, and for a mean word, a venomous one..."

"But can you do anything for her, Doctor?" the parents asked.

"Do anything? Well, that's easy! My dear monsieur, I am honoured to ask for your daughter's hand in marriage."

"You want to marry her?"

"If she will accept me, yes I do."

"But why?" her mother asked. "Do you think that marriage will cure her?"

"I very much hope not!" replied the doctor. "You see, I work at the Pasteur Institute, developing venom antidotes. We're rather short of snakes in my department. A young lady like your daughter is like a whole chest of pearls to me!"

So Marie married the young doctor. He was very good to her, and made her as happy as she could be while living with such a problem. From time to time, when he asked her, she said dreadful words so as to provide him with an adder or a cobra, or a coral snake—and the rest of the time she did not speak at all, which, luckily, did not bother her too much, for she was a simple, modest young lady.

Sometime later, the fairy in the tap wanted to find out what had happened to the two girls. She popped out to see their parents one Saturday evening after midnight, when they had come back from the cinema and were having a snack before going to bed. The fairy asked them about their daughters and they told her everything. Quite bewildered, she learnt that not only had she rewarded the bad daughter and punished the good one, but that, out of pure chance, the bad gift had turned out to Marie's advantage, while the gift of the pearls had become a terrible curse for poor Martine and she had been punished far beyond what she deserved. Disheartened, the poor fairy said to herself:

"I'd have done better to sit tight and do nothing. I don't have a clue how the world works these days; I get everything wrong and I can't even foresee the consequences of my own actions. I must go and find a wizard who is wiser than me, so he will marry me and I can obey him. But where shall I look?"

Pondering this question, the fairy went out into the street, and she was fluttering along the pavement on rue Broca, when she saw a shop with its lights still on. It was Papa Sayeed's cafe-grocer's. Papa Sayeed himself was just putting all the chairs on the tables before going to bed.

The door was closed, but by making herself very tiny, the fairy was able to squeeze in under it. For she had spied, lying on a shelf, a great notebook and pencil case, which Bashir had forgotten to put away.

When Papa Sayeed had gone to bed, the fairy tore a page out of the notebook (have you noticed that there is often a page missing from Bashir's notebooks?). Next she took some coloured pencils out of the pencil case and began to draw. Of course, Papa Sayeed had turned out the lights when he went to bed. But fairies have good eyesight and can even see colours in the middle of the night. So the tap fairy drew a wizard with a tall pointed hat and a long, black cloak. When the drawing was finished, she blew on it and began to sing:

Wizard of night
Seen without light
Traced by this fairy
Oh won't you marry me?

The wizard's face twitched and winced:

"No, I'd rather not," he said, "you are too fat."

"Then too bad for you!" retorted the fairy.

She blew on him again and the wizard stopped moving. She tore out another page (sometimes there are several pages missing in Bashir's notebooks) and drew another wizard, with a grey cloak this time.

She blew on this drawing and asked:

Wizard drawn
The colour of dawn
Traced by this fairy
Oh won't you marry me?

But the grey wizard looked down to avoid her eyes:

"No, thanks. You're far too skinny."

"That's your loss, then!"

The fairy blew on him again and once more he was nothing but a mere pencil drawing. Next she looked through the coloured pencils and realized there was only one she had not yet tried: the blue one. All the other coloured pencils had been lost!

"This time," she thought, "I mustn't mess it up!"

So, she took a third sheet of paper and, taking great care, drew a third wizard, this time with a blue cloak. When she had finished she gazed at him lovingly. Truly, this one was the handsomest of them all!

"Let's hope he likes me!" she thought.

The fairy blew on him and began once more to sing:

Wizard of sunrise
Blue as the clear skies
Traced by this fairy
Oh won't you marry me?

"Certainly," said the wizard.

Then the fairy blew on him three times. At her third breath, the two-dimensional wizard thickened and then stepped out of the piece of paper. When at last he was standing upright, he took the fairy by the hand and the pair of them went out through the door and flew away down the street.

"Most importantly," said the blue wizard, "I will take away Martine's gift as well as Marie's."

"Will you really?" asked the fairy.

"It's the very first thing to do," he said.

There and then he recited a magical formula.

The next morning, Martine had stopped speaking in pearls. Realizing this, at first the apparently charming young man gave her a beating. Then, when he saw this wasn't helping, he threw her out of his house. Martine went back to her parents, but the adventure had been a lesson to her and, from that day on, she was quite sweet and good.

*

On the same day, Marie stopping speaking snakes. This was a shame for the Pasteur Institute, but Marie's husband was not a bit sorry, for now he had the pleasure of talking to her, and he realized that she was as intelligent as she was good.

The wizard and the fairy disappeared. I know that they are still around, but I don't know where. They hardly do miracles any more, being very, very cautious these days, and they don't mind in the least if anybody knows about them.

I almost forgot to add this: opening up the shop on the day after this memorable night, Madame Sayeed, Bashir's mother, found her son's pencils scattered all over a shelf, his big notebook open with three pages torn out and, on two of the pages, drawings of wizards. Very cross, she called her son and said severely:

"What is this mess? Aren't you ashamed? You think we buy you all these notebooks so you can do this?"

However hard Bashir protested that it wasn't his fault, nobody believed him.

The Witch in the Broom Cupboard

It's Monsieur Pierre writing here, and now I'm going to tell you a story about something that really happened to me.

Rummaging in my pocket one day, I found a five-franc coin. I thought to myself:

"Hurray! I'm rich! Now I can buy myself a house!"

And I hurried off to see a solicitor:

"Good morning, monsieur. Would you happen to have a house to sell for about five francs?"

"Five francs? No, I'm terribly sorry," said the solicitor, "I haven't got one for that price. I have houses at twenty francs, at fifty francs, at a hundred francs, but nothing at five francs."

I asked again, just to be sure:

"Really? Might we not find one if we looked very hard... Not even a very small house?"

And then, the solicitor slapped his forehead:

"Now you mention it, I may have something! Just a moment..."

He rummaged through his files and pulled out a folder:

"Look, here you go: a neat little house on the high street, with one bedroom, kitchen, bathroom, living room, toilet and broom cupboard. "

"How much is it?"

"Three francs fifty. With my fees on top, it will come to five francs exactly."

"That's perfect. I'll take it."

Proudly, I laid my five-franc coin down on the desk. The solicitor took it and held out a contract.

"Here you go, please sign here. And put your initials there. And there. And there too."

I signed everywhere and handed back the contract, saying:

"Is this all right?"

He replied:

"Quite right. He he he he!"

I stared at him, intrigued:

112

"What are you laughing for?"

"Oh, nothing, nothing... Haha!"

I didn't much like that laugh. It was a nervous little laugh, the laugh of someone who has just played a mean trick on you. I asked again:

"This house does exist, doesn't it?"

"Absolutely! Heh heh heh!"

"And is it well built? The roof isn't about to come down on my head, is it?"

"Hoho! Certainly not!"

"In that case, what's so funny?"

"Nothing at all, like I said! Anyway, here; have the key. You can go and see for yourself... Good luck! Hoo hoo hoo!"

I took the key and left to go and see the house. It was indeed a very pretty little house, smartly fitted, bright and airy, with a bedroom, kitchen, bathroom, living room, toilet and broom cupboard. When I had looked into every room, I said to myself:

"What about a quick hello to my new neighbours?"

Okay, let's get going! I went to knock on my neighbour's door to the left.

"Hello neighbour! I'm your new neighbour on the right. I've just bought the little house with a bedroom, kitchen, bathroom, living room, toilet and broom cupboard."

Hearing this, the good man turned as white as a sheet, before my eyes. He looked at me with a horrified expression, and *bam*! Without a word, he slammed the door in my face. I thought to myself, charitably:

"Well! Quite an eccentric!"

And I went to knock on the door of my right-hand neighbour:

"Hello neighbour! I'm your new neighbour on the left. I'm the one who's just bought the little house with a bedroom, kitchen, bathroom, living room, toilet and broom cupboard."

At which, there on the doorstep, the old lady clasped her hands, gazed at me with great compassion and began a long lament.

"Alas, my poor m'sieur, yer quite through yer luck today! Oh, 'n it's a pitiful thing to see, a kin' young man like yerself! Well, Lord willin' yer'll come through it sum'ow... Long as yer've life, yer've 'ope, as they say, an' long as yer 'ave yer 'ealf..."

Hearing this, I began to grow nervous:

"But really, my dear madame, can you at least

tell me what's wrong? Everyone I talk to about the house—"

But the old lady interrupted me instantly:

"I 'ope yer'll excuse me, my dear m'sieur, but I've me roast in the oven... I must be off 'n see it don't burn!"

Bam! She too slammed the door in my face.

This time, I was angry. I went back to the solicitor and said to him:

"Now you'd better tell me what's so amusing about my house, so I can join in the fun. And if you don't wish to tell me, rest assured that I will split your head in two!"

With these words, I raised his big glass ashtray, menacingly. This time the bloke stopped laughing:

"Now, now, gently does it! Calm yourself, my dear monsieur! Please put that down and take a seat."

"First you can do some explaining!"

"But of course, I'll explain. After all, now you've signed the contract, I might as well tell you... the house is haunted!"

"Haunted? Haunted by whom?"

"By the witch in the broom cupboard!"

"Couldn't you have told me earlier?"

"Not at all! If I'd told you, you wouldn't have wanted to buy the house, and I wanted to sell it. He he he!"

"Enough giggling, or I'll crack your head open!"

"All right, all right..."

"But tell me, now I think about it: I looked into the broom cupboard, less than fifteen minutes ago... I didn't see any witch in there."

"That's because she's not there in the daytime. She only comes out at night."

"And what does she do there, during the night?"

"Oh, she keeps to herself, she doesn't make any noise, she just stays there, quite well behaved, in her cupboard... only beware! If you should have the misfortune to sing:

Witchy witch, beware,
Watch out for your derrière!

"Then she'll come out... and it'll be your turn to watch out!"

Hearing this, I leapt to my feet, shouting:

"You idiot! You'd no need to go singing that for me. It would never have crossed my mind to sing such tosh. Now, I'll never be able to get it out of my head!"

"That's the idea! He he he!"

And, just as I lunged for his neck, the solicitor escaped through a small door hidden behind him.

What could I do? I went back home, thinking:

"After all, I only have to be a little careful... Let's try to forget that idiotic rhyme!"

Easier said than done, for words like those are not easily forgotten. For the first few months, of course, I was on my guard. Then, after a year and a half, I was comfortable in the house, I had grown used to it, it was familiar... So I began to hum the tune during the day, when the witch wouldn't be there... And then, outside, where I was in no danger... And then I started singing it at night, in the house—but not the whole rhyme! I only sang the beginning:

Witchy witch, beware...

And then I would stop. When I did that, I sometimes thought I saw the door to the broom cupboard begin to shake... But since I always stopped at that point, the witch couldn't do a thing. Realizing this, I began to sing a little bit more each day: *Watch out...* then *Watch out for...* and then *Watch out for your de...* and even *Watch out for your derri...* I would stop just in time! There was no doubt about it, the cupboard door was shaking, rattling, on the verge of coming open... The witch must have been furious in there!

This little game went on until last Christmas. That night, after having Christmas Eve supper with friends, I came home, a little tipsy, just as the clock was striking four in the morning, singing to myself all the way:

> *Witchy witch, beware,*
> *Watch out for your derrière!*

Of course, I wasn't running any real risk, for I was outside the house. I reached the high street: *Witchy witch, beware...* I stopped outside my front door: *Watch out for your derrière!...* I took the key from my pocket: *Witchy witch, beware...* I was still in no danger... I slid the key into the lock: *Watch out for your derrière...* I turned it, went in, took the key out again, closed the door behind me, went down the corridor, towards the stairs...

Witchy witch, beware,
Watch out for your derrière!

Blast! I'd done it now! This time I'd sung the whole rhyme! And then I heard, very close by, a shrill, mean, nasty little voice:

"Oh really! And why exactly should I be looking out for my *derrière*?"

It was her. The broom-cupboard door was open and the witch was standing on the threshold, her right hand on her hip and one of my brooms held in her left. Naturally, I tried to explain:

"Oh, I'm so sorry, madame! A moment of distraction... I forgot... I mean, I meant to say... I hummed it without thinking..."

She chuckled softly:

"Without thinking? Liar! For two years now, that song is all you've been thinking about. You made a fine fool of me, didn't you, stopping every time just before the last word, the last syllable, even! But I said to myself: 'Patience, my pretty! One day, he'll spit it all out, his little sing-song, from start to finish, and when that day comes it will be my turn to have some fun...' And here we are. The day has come!"

I fell to my knees and began to plead:

"Have pity, madame! Don't hurt me! I didn't mean to offend you: I actually really like witches. Some of my best friends are witches! My poor mother was a witch! If she weren't dead, she could tell you herself... And besides, today is Christmas Day! Little Baby Jesus was born tonight. You can't make me disappear today, of all days..."

The witch replied:

"Taratata! I won't listen to a word! But since you've got such a ready tongue, I'm going to set you a challenge: you have three days in which to ask me for three things. Three impossible things! If I can give you all three of them, you're mine. But if I am unable to give you any one of the three things, I shall disappear for ever and you'll never see me again. So, I'm listening!"

Playing for time, I replied:

"Hm, I don't know... I've no idea... I'll have to think about this one... Can I have today to think about it?"

"Fine," said the witch. "I'm in no rush. See you in the evening!"

And she disappeared.

Sitting in thought for several hours, I cudgelled,

wrestled with and generally racked my brains—when suddenly I remembered that my friend Bashir had two little fish in a bowl, and that he had said these two little fish were in fact *magic* fish. Without losing another second, I raced down rue Broca to go and ask Bashir:

"Have you still got your two little fish?"

"Yes. Why?"

"Because there's a witch in my house, a really old, wicked witch. I have to ask her for something impossible by tonight. If I don't, she'll spirit me away. Do you think your little fish might give me an idea?"

"Sure they will," said Bashir. "I'll go and get them."

He went into the back of his father's shop and came back with a bowl full of water in which two little fish were swimming, one red and the other yellow with black spots. They really did look like magic fish.

"Now, speak to them!"

"I can't!" Bashir replied. "*I* can't talk to them; they don't understand French. We need an interpreter! But don't worry—we have one here."

And my friend Bashir began to sing:

Little mouse
Little friend
Will you come this way?
Speak to my little fish
And you shall have a tasty dish!

Hardly had he finished singing when an adorable little grey mouse came trotting out onto the counter, sat down on her little bottom beside the fishbowl and gave three tiny squeaks, like this:

"Eep! Eep! Eep!"

Bashir translated:

"She says she's ready. Tell her what happened to you."

I bent down and told the mouse everything: all about the solicitor, the house, the neighbours, the cupboard, the song, the witch and the challenge she had set me. After listening to me in silence, the mouse turned to the little fish and said to them in her language:

"Eepi eepeepi peepi reepeeteepi..."

And on like that for another five minutes.

*

Once they too had listened in silence, the fish exchanged glances, consulted, whispered in each other's ears, and then finally, the red fish rose to the surface of the water and opened his mouth several times, making a tiny, almost inaudible sound:

"Po—po—po—po..."

And so on, for nearly a minute.

When that was done, the little mouse turned back to Bashir and began squeaking again:

"Peepiri peepi reepipi."

I asked Bashir:

"What is she saying?"

He replied:

"This evening, when you see the witch, ask her for jewels made of rubber that shine like real gemstones. She won't be able to bring you any."

I thanked Bashir. Bashir dropped a few water-fleas into the bowl for the fish to eat and gave the mouse a round of salami, and I left the shop to go back home.

The witch was waiting for me in the corridor:

"So? What will you ask me for?"

I replied, confidently:

"I want you to give me jewels made of rubber that shine like real gemstones!"

But the witch began to laugh:

"Haha! You didn't think up that one by yourself! But never mind, here they are."

She rummaged about inside her bodice and pulled out a fistful of jewellery: two bracelets, three rings and a necklace, all shining just like gold, glittering like diamonds, in all the colours of the rainbow—and soft as the rubber in your pencil case!"

"See you tomorrow for your second request," said the witch. "And this time, try to make it a little more challenging!"

And—*pouf*! She disappeared.

The following morning, I took the jewellery with me to a friend who is a chemist, and asked him:

"Can you tell me what this substance is?"

"Give me a minute," he said.

And he locked himself up in his lab. After an hour, he came back out, saying:

"This is quite extraordinary! They're made of rubber! I've never seen such a thing. May I keep them?"

I left the jewellery with him and went back to see Bashir.

"The jewellery was no good," I told him. "The witch brought them to me straight away."

"In that case, we'll have to try again," said Bashir.

He went back to get the fishbowl, set it on the counter and began to sing once more:

Little mouse
Little friend
Will you come this way?
Speak to my little fish
And you shall have a tasty dish!

The little mouse ran out, I told her what had happened, she translated, then listened to the reply from the fish and transmitted it to Bashir:

"Peepi pirreepipi ippee ippee ip!"

"What does she say?"

And Bashir translated for me, again:

"Ask the witch for a branch from the macaroni tree, and replant it in your garden to see if it will grow!"

That very evening, I said to the witch:

"Bring me a branch from the macaroni tree!"

"Haha! That's not your own idea either! But no matter: here you go."

And *pouf!* She pulled a magnificent branch of flowering macaroni out of her bodice, with twigs made of spaghetti and long noodle leaves, pasta-shell flowers. It even had little seeds shaped like alphabet pasta!

I was quite amazed, but even so, I couldn't let the witch off so easily:

"That isn't a branch from a real tree—it won't grow!"

"That's what you think," said the witch. "Just plant it out in your garden and you'll see. Catch you tomorrow evening!"

Without further ado, I went into the garden, dug a small hole in a flower bed, planted the macaroni branch in it, watered it and went to bed. The following morning, I went downstairs to look. The branch had grown huge: it was almost a whole new tree, with several fresh branches and twice as many flowers. I gripped it with both hands and tried to pull it up... but I couldn't! I scratched at the ground around the trunk and I saw that it was being held tight to the ground by hundreds of its own tiny vermicelli roots...

This time I was desperate. I didn't even feel like going back to Bashir. I wandered around like a soul in pain, and I'm sure I saw people whispering when they saw me go by. I knew what they were saying, too!

"That poor young man—just look at him! It's his last day on this earth, you can see straight away. The witch will surely carry him away tonight!"

On the stroke of midday, Bashir gave me a call:

"So? Did it work?"

"No, it didn't. I am lost. The witch is going to carry me off tonight. Goodbye, Bashir!"

"Not at all, nothing is lost. Why are you going on like this? Come round here right now and we'll ask the little fish!"

"What for? It's no good."

"And what good is doing nothing? I'm telling you, come to my place right away! It's shameful to give up like this!"

"All right, if you wish, I'm coming..."

And I went back to Bashir's house. When I got there, everything was ready: Bashir, the bowl with the little fish and the little mouse sitting beside it.

For the third time I told my story, the little mouse translated it, the fish discussed it at length, and this time it was the yellow fish that came to the surface to speak in a series of gulps:

"Po—po—po—po—po—po—po..."

He went on for nearly a quarter of an hour.

Next the mouse turned back to us and made a whole speech, which took a good ten minutes.

I asked Bashir:

"What on earth can they be going on about, this time?"

Bashir told me:

"Listen, and do pay attention because this is not so simple. This evening, when you get back home, ask the witch to bring you the *hairy frog*. She will be very embarrassed, for the hairy frog is in fact the witch herself! The witch is no more, no less, than the hairy frog in human form. Now, one of two things should happen: either she won't be able to bring you the hairy frog, in which case she will have to leave your house for ever—or she will decide to show you the frog anyway, and to do that, she will have to transform herself back into it. As soon as she has turned into the hairy frog, you must catch her and tie her up good and tight with thick string. Then she won't be able to grow back into the witch again. After that, you must shave her hair off and then you'll be left with a perfectly inoffensive, ordinary frog."

Now I began to feel hopeful again. I asked Bashir:

"Could you sell me the string?"

Bashir sold me a ball of tough string. I thanked him and went back home.

Come evening, the witch was there, waiting for me:

"So, my pretty, has the time come for me to spirit you away? What are you going to ask me for now?"

I made sure that the string was nice and loose in my pocket, and then I replied:

"Bring me the hairy frog!"

Now the witch stopped laughing. She gave a shriek of rage:

"What? What did you say? You didn't think this one up by yourself either! Ask me for something else!"

But I stood firm:

"Why should I ask for something else? I don't want anything else; I want the hairy frog!"

"You have no right to ask me for that!"

"Is it that you *can't* bring me the hairy frog?"

"Of course I can, but this isn't fair!"

"So you don't want to bring it to me?"

"No, I don't want to!"

"In that case, go back where you came from. This is my home!"

At that, the witch began to screech:

"Oh, it's like that, is it? In that case, here you go, since this is what you want; you shall have your hairy frog!"

And before my eyes she began to grow smaller, to dwindle, shrivel and shrink as if she were melting away, so much and so completely that within five minutes there before me was nothing but a fat, green frog with a thick crop of hair on her head, hopping around on the floor and croaking as if she had hiccups:

"Ribbit, ribbit! Ribbit, ribbit!"

I jumped on her right away and pinned her to the ground. Pulling the string from my pocket, I took her and trussed her up like a chunk of salami... She wriggled, almost strangling herself; she did her best to grow back into the witch... but the string was too tight! Her eyes bulged furiously at me, while she croaked desperately:

"Ribbit, ribbit! Ribbit! Ribbit!"

puic Rosaba

Without hesitating, I carried the frog into the bathroom, soaped her up and shaved her hair off, after which I untied her, ran a little water into the bath and left her to spend the night there.

The next morning, I took her to Bashir in a small bowl with a tiny ladder inside it, so she could help forecast the weather for him (she would climb up the ladder if good weather was coming and sit at the bottom if the forecast was bad). Bashir thanked me and put the new bowl on a shelf, next to the one with the little fish.

Since that day, the two fish and the frog have not stopped talking to each other. The frog says: "Ribbit, ribbit!" and the fish: "Po—po!" and they go on like that for days on end!

One day I said to Bashir:

"How about you call the mouse in, so we can find out what they're saying to each other?"

"Sure, if you like!" Bashir said.

And once more, he sang:

> *Little mouse*
> *Little friend*
> *Will you come this way...*

When the mouse came, Bashir asked her to listen and translate. But this time, the mouse refused point blank.

"Why won't she translate?" I asked.

Bashir replied:

"Because it's nothing but swearing!"

So now you know the story of the witch in the broom cupboard. And now, if you come and visit me in my little house, whether by day or by night, you can quite safely sing:

Witchy witch, beware,
Watch out for your derrière!

I promise nothing will happen to you!

fin

The Good Little Devil

There was once a charming little devil who was red all over, with two little black horns and two bat-wings. His daddy was a big green devil and his mother a black she-devil. All three of them lived together in a place called Hell, which can be found right in the centre of Planet Earth.

Hell is not like how it is round here. Indeed, it's quite the opposite: everything that here we think is good, is considered bad in Hell; and everything that here we think is bad, is considered good down there. This is why, officially, devils are supposed to be wicked. For them, it's good to be bad.

But *our* little devil, well he wanted to be *good*, and so he was the despair of his whole family.

Every evening when he came home from school, his father would ask him:

"What did you do today?"

"I went to school."

"What an idiot! Had you done all your homework?"

"Yes, Papa."

"What a dummy! Had you learnt your lessons?"

"Yes, Papa."

"Miserable child! You have at least, I hope, wasted a few hours?"

"Mmm..."

"Did you fight with any of your little schoolfriends?"

"No, Papa."

"Did you flick some balls of soggy paper at them while the teacher wasn't looking?"

"No, Papa."

"You didn't even think of putting drawing pins on your teacher's chair so that he pricked his bottom when he sat down?"

"No, Papa."

"In that case, what *did* you do?"

"Well, I did a dictation, two maths problems, a bit of history, some geography..."

Hearing this, the poor daddy devil held his horns in both hands, as if he felt like tearing them out, and shook his head:

"What did I do to deserve such a child? When I think of the years your mother and I have spent, what we sacrificed to give you a bad education, to set you a bad example, to help you grow up into a fine, tall and wicked devil! But no! Instead of giving in to temptation, this young gentleman has to cause trouble! In fact, let's think seriously: what would you like to do when you're grown up?"

"I'd like to be nice," replied the little devil.

Of course, his mother wept and his father punished him. But there was nothing to be done: the little devil stuck to his plan. In the end, his father told him:

"My poor child, I despair of you. I would have liked you to grow up to be Someone, but I see now that it's impossible. Only this week, you came top in maths! In view of this, I have decided to take you out of school and make you an apprentice. You shall never be worse than a minor imp, a mere boiler-room stove-stoker... A shame for you, but it is your own fault!

Indeed, the very next day, the little devil stopped going to school. His father sent him off to be an apprentice in the Grand Central Heating System, where he was assigned to look after the fire beneath a great cauldron in which about twenty people (who had been very, very wicked when they were alive) were boiling and bubbling away for ever.

But even here the little devil did not satisfy his masters. He was friendly with the poor damned people and, every time he saw a chance, he would let the fire burn a bit lower so that they wouldn't be quite so hot in there. He chatted to them and told them funny stories to distract them—or he would ask them questions such as:

"Why are you here?"

To which they would reply: we killed people, or, we stole things; we did this, we did that.

"And what if you were to think very hard about our dear Lord?" the little devil would ask. "Don't you feel that sometimes that could help things turn out all right?"

"Alas, no!" they said. "Once we get here, we're in here for ever!"

"Never mind that, try thinking of him a little, when you're not too hot..."

They did think of him, and there were even a

few among them who, having thought about God for some minutes, actually disappeared all of a sudden—pop!—like a soap bubble. They were never seen again. For the kind Lord had pardoned them.

This went on until, one day, the Grand High Controller of the Diabolical Cauldrons came round on his annual inspection. And when he came to our little devil's cauldron, he kicked up an ungodly fuss!

"What in Hell is going on here? This cauldron should contain twenty-one people but I can only see eighteen! What does this mean? And the fire has practically gone out! What kind of work is this? I see, this isn't Hell any longer, it's the French Riviera now, is it? Right, hop to it, this second, let's have you blowing on those coals and get it boiling right up! And as for you, my little friend (he was speaking to our young devil now), as for you, since you are not capable of keeping up a basic fire, we shall have to put you to work at the coalface!"

The following day, the little devil was put to work in a coal mine. They gave him a pickaxe, and he spent his days digging tunnels and knocking out great chunks of coal. This time, everyone was pleased, for he was a hard worker. Of course, he knew that this coal was destined for the cauldrons' fires, but it was just the way he was: when he went to do something, he could not help but do it well.

One day, while digging along a new seam of anthracite, the little devil made one lucky blow with his pickaxe and all of a sudden he was bathed in light. He peered into the hole he had made and saw a great, brightly lit, underground cavern, with a platform full of busy people, getting in and out of a little green train with a red carriage. He had found the underground!

"Great!" thought the little devil. "Now I've found some humans! They'll surely help me to be good!"

He squeezed through his hole and jumped down onto the platform. But hardly had they caught sight of him than the humans began to run away, screaming horribly. As it was rush hour, there was a terrible scrum: children were squashed and women were stepped on. The little devil did his best to reassure them, calling:

"Please stay! Don't be afraid!"

But he could not make himself heard, for the humans were shouting even more loudly.

In ten minutes' time, the station was empty, except for the dead and the injured. Not knowing quite what to do, the little devil went straight on ahead, climbing up one staircase, then another; he pushed through a door and soon found himself in the street. But the firemen waiting for him there hosed him down brutally with their fire hose. He tried to escape down the other side of the road, but policemen ran straight for him, waving their truncheons. He tried to fly away, but the police helicopters already had him in their lights. Luckily, right there at the edge of the pavement, he spotted an open drain and into this he plunged.

The little devil spent the whole day wandering through underground passages full of filthy water. Only after midnight did he return to ground level, where he went on walking through small, dark streets, thinking to himself:

"I still need to find someone to help me out! How can I make them believe that I'm not wicked?"

As he was thinking this, an old lady appeared, scurrying along the pavement. The devil went up to her, tugged gently at her sleeve and enquired sweetly:

"Madame..."

The old lady turned to look at him:

"What is it, little boy? Why aren't you tucked up in bed, at this late hour?"

"Madame," said the little devil, "I want to be good. What should I do?"

But just then, looking more closely, the old lady caught sight of his two little horns and his bat-wings. She began to stammer:

"No! No! Have pity, Lord! I shan't do it again!"

"What won't you do again?" asked the little devil.

But the old lady did not reply. She had fainted away in the street.

"My bad luck," thought the devil. "And she seemed so nice at first..."

He walked on a bit farther and, a little way down rue Broca, he caught sight of a cafe with a few lights still on. He hurried towards it and, through the glass-paned door, he saw Papa Sayeed, who had just locked up and was preparing to go to bed. Shyly, the devil tapped on the glass:

"Excuse me, monsieur..."

"Too late! We're closed!" said Papa Sayeed.

"But I was hoping..."

"I'm telling you we're closed!"

"But I don't want anything to drink, I just want to be good!"

"You're too late! Come back tomorrow."

The little devil was desperate. He was beginning to wonder if he wouldn't be better off going back to Hell and learning to be wicked like everybody else when, suddenly, he heard a man's steps approaching.

"This is my last chance," he thought.

He half-ran, half-flew towards the sound and stopped at the corner of the boulevard. A dark figure was advancing to meet him. It looked like a woman, but it was making great strides, like a soldier. In fact it was a priest, dressed in his long cassock, coming back from visiting a sick person. The little devil spoke up:

"Excuse me, monsieur..."

"Excuse *me?*"

The priest took one look at the little devil and seemed to have a big shock, then he made a series of very odd gestures in front of his face at top speed, while muttering a string of Latin words, not one of which our little devil understood.

Since the devil was polite, he waited until the priest had finished his little game, then spoke up again:

"Excuse me, monsieur. I am a young devil and I'd like to grow up to be good. What should I do?"

Amazed, the priest stared at him:

"You're asking me what you should do?"

"Yes, so as to grow up good. What should I do, at my age, to become good?"

"You have to obey your parents," said the priest, without thinking.

"But I can't, monsieur. My parents want me to grow up wicked!"

Now the priest began to understand.

"Oh yes. Bother. Of course they do!" he exclaimed. "But what a spot you're in! This is the first I've ever heard of such a case... You are sincere, I take it?"

"Oh yes, monsieur!"

"I don't even know if I'm allowed to believe you... Listen, in any event, your situation is much too serious for me to judge by myself. You must go and consult the Pope in Rome."

"Right away, monsieur. Thank you so much, monsieur."

And off the little devil flew.

He travelled all night and only arrived in Rome the following morning. As luck would have it, while

146

flying over the Vatican, he saw the Pope praying alone in his garden. The little devil flew down and landed beside him.

"Excuse me, Mr Pope..."

The Pope turned round and glared at him, angrily.

"Go away," he said. "I didn't ask for *you*."

"I know you didn't, Mr Pope. But, I need you to help me! I want to be good. How should I do it?"

The Pope was looking crosser and crosser.

"You? Be good? Get out of here! You're just trying to tempt me!"

"But I assure you I'm not!" cried the little devil. "Why reject me before you know the truth? And what danger is there in simply giving me some advice?"

"That's true," said the Pope, more calmly. "After all, there's no harm done by a bit of advice. Well then, sit down and tell me your story. And take care not to lie!"

The devil launched straight in and told the whole story of his life, from the beginning. As he spoke, the Pope's suspicions melted away like snow in the sun. At the end of his tale, the Holy Father was almost weeping.

"What a beautiful story!" he murmured, his voice full of emotion. "Almost too beautiful to be true! It really is the first time, to my knowledge, that such a thing has occurred... Indeed, in that case, I expect that God himself is behind it! My dear, I have only one piece of advice for you and that is: speak directly to God. I am only a man and my work is only with human problems."

"I have to go and find the Good Lord?"

"That would be the best thing to do."

"How should I do it?"

"Well, that's easy enough. You have wings, don't you?"

"Yes."

"In that case, fly as high as you can, without thinking about anything in particular, simply singing a song that I will teach you. This is the song that helps us find heaven."

And softly the Pope sang a song, a brief little song, very short and simple but very, very beautiful. Don't ask me to sing it to you, for if I knew it, I wouldn't be here—I would be in heaven too.

When the devil had learnt the song by heart, he thanked the Pope and flew away. He flew as high as he could, thinking of nothing in particular, but singing the magical song over and over without stopping.

And indeed, he had hardly sung it through three times before there appeared a great white door with a man sitting in front of it, an old bearded man wearing a blue toga and with a halo over his head, holding a bunch of keys. This was Saint Peter.

"Whoa there! Where do you think you're off to like that?"

"I would like to speak to the Good Lord."

"To the Good Lord Himself! Is that all you're after? With those horns and that pair of wings? Have you not had a glance in the mirror recently?"

"But the Pope in Rome sent me!"

This time, Saint Peter was rattled. He looked hard at the little devil, frowning, then began to grumble:

"The Pope this, the Pope that... Why's he getting mixed up in this, now?... Anyway, since you're here, you can sit our heavenly entrance exams. Do you know how to read and write? Can you count?"

"Yes, yes I can!"

"I don't believe a word! You can't have done a stroke of work at school!"

"Excuse me, but I did do my schoolwork!"

"Really! What's two plus two?"

"Four."

"Are you sure? How do you know?"

"I just know..."

"Hm! A lucky guess!... Well, do you want to take our exams or not?"

"I do want to, sir."

"Really, you're sure you do?"

"Yes, sir."

"You're not afraid?"

"No, sir."

"Right, as you wish! Come this way. You can see, down there, that's the great courtyard. The first door on the right, there: that's little Jesus's office. He'll oversee the reading test."

"Thank you, sir."

The devil went in through a grand doorway and found himself facing the great courtyard. It was just like a schoolyard, with a covered walkway all around it. Through the arches he could see a number of tall, green, glass-paned doors. The first door on the right had a copper plaque on it, inscribed as follows:

LITTLE JESUS

Son of God

Enter without knocking

The devil opened the door and found himself in a classroom. Little Jesus was sitting at the teacher's desk. He was a blond-haired child, wearing a rough cloth tunic, also with a halo over his head but a much prettier one than Saint Peter's.

"Come in, come in!" he said.

"Little Jesus," said the devil. "I have come—"

"No need to say, I know why. You've come to take the reading test?"

"Yes, Little Jesus."

"In that case, come here, and read this."

The little devil went over to him and Little Jesus held out an open book. But when the devil began to leaf through it, he saw that all the pages were blank.

"Now, read!" said Little Jesus.

The devil looked at the book, then back at Little Jesus to see if he was teasing. But no: he was quite serious.

"Well, I'm listening. Do you know how to read or not?"

The devil looked at the book once more and protested:

"But there's nothing written in it—all the pages are blank."

And as he said this, the words he was pronouncing wrote themselves out along the left page in big capital letters: BUT THERE'S NOTHING WRITTEN IN IT—ALL THE PAGES ARE BLANK.

"Let me see," said Little Jesus.

He took the book back and read from it under his breath:

"But there's nothing written in it: all the pages are blank."

Then he looked up and gave the devil a broad grin.

"Ten out of ten."

"So I passed the exam?" asked the devil.

"Now, now. Don't get carried away! You have passed the reading test. Now you must go through to the next room, which belongs to the Good Lord, my father. He will give you the writing test. Off you go!"

"Goodbye, Little Jesus," said the devil. "And thank you!"

"Goodbye."

The devil left the room, turned right again and stopped in front of the next door. This door had a silver plaque, on which the following was inscribed:

GOOD LORD
Twenty-four hour opening
Enter without knocking

The devil went in. This second classroom was much like the first, only a good deal smaller. The Good Lord was also sitting at a teacher's desk. He was a handsome old man in a red cloak with a long white beard and a double halo over his head. The little devil began to speak:

"Good Lord, sir..."

"Pointless, my dear, I know everything. My son has sent you here to take the writing test."

"Yes, sir..."

"Not a word now. Sit down, we shall do a dictation."

The little devil sat down at a table. On it were a fountain pen and some paper. He picked up the pen, dipped it in his inkwell and waited.

"Are you ready?" asked the Good Lord. "I'll begin now."

The little devil leant over his paper and... didn't hear a word. After a moment, he looked up again. He saw that the Good Lord was moving his lips, but not making any sound at all.

"Excuse me, Good Lord, sir..."

"I pray you not to interrupt me. What is it?"

"I can't hear you."

"Really? In that case, I'll start again."

And the Good Lord began once more to move his lips without making any sound at all. Then, since the devil remained motionless where he was, the Lord stopped and reproached him gravely:

"Now, then, what are you waiting for? Don't you know how to write?"

"I do, I do, but..."

"Fine, so I'll say it all over for the third time. But if you don't write anything, you'll get a zero!"

And he began his silent performance just as before.

"Well, this is just too bad," the little devil thought to himself, "I'll have to write something, no matter what."

And he began to write, with all the care he could muster:

Dear Good Lord,

I am very sorry, for I cannot hear a word of what you're saying. Nevertheless, since I must write something, I am taking this opportunity to tell you

that I love you very much, that I would like to be
good so as to stay near you, even if I can only be
the lowest of your angels.

LITTLE DEVIL

"Have you finished?" asked the Good Lord.

"Yes, sir."

"Well, hand it in, then."

The Good Lord took the sheet of paper, read it, raised his eyebrows and began to chuckle:

"So it turns out to be true, you do know how to write!"

"Have I passed the exams then?"

"Not so fast, young man! The hardest test is still to come. You must go through to the next room, which belongs to my mother, for the maths test. Pay close attention, for my mother is strict. Now, get along with you!"

"Thank you, Good Lord!"

On the third door there was a gold plaque with the following inscription:

VIRGIN MARY
Mother of God
Queen of Heaven
Knock before Entering

The devil gave two small taps. A woman's voice answered him:

"Enter."

This room, too, was a classroom, but an absolutely tiny one, minuscule, containing only one table and the teacher's desk. Naturally, the mother of God was sitting at the desk. She was wearing a long blue dress and had a magnificent, three-tiered halo. The little devil was so nervous that he didn't dare say a word.

"Sit down," said the Virgin Mary.

She gave him a sheet of paper, a fountain pen and some coloured pencils, and told him:

"Now, pay attention! Your task is to find a three-figure number that can be divided by three, and that has blue eyes and one leg shorter than the other. I'll be back in ten minutes. If, in ten minutes' time, you've not found this number, then you've failed and we'll have to send you away."

And she left the room.

Now the little devil felt really lost. And yet, once again, he did not want to sit and do nothing, so he decided:

"I could still start by looking for three-figure numbers that can be divided by three. That will surely be better than nothing..."

Perhaps you know this already: a number can be divided by three when the total of all its digits added together can itself be divided by three. The little devil began to write down a long list of these three-digit numbers, one after the other:

123, 543, 624, 525, 282, 771, 189, 222, etc.

Then he looked hard at them, while allowing his mind to wander, and all of a sudden, going back to the number 189, he noticed something:

He noticed that number 189 had a belly and a head, and even two legs. The head was the top circle of the 8 and the belly, its bottom circle. As for the two legs, they were the 1 and the 9—and one leg was longer than the other, for the tail of the 9 came down below the line where the 1 ended.

Now the little devil cut his piece of paper into two, and on the blank half he drew a lovely, big number 189, with the 8 a little higher than the other two digits. Now he had only to draw two blue eyes in the 8's top circle, which he did right away. While he was at it, he added a little red mouth, a small nose and two ears. He had just finished his drawing when the Mother of God came back in:

"Well? Have you found the number?"

She came over, looked at the little devil's drawing and began to laugh:

"Oh! But this is very nicely done!"

She took the half-sheet of paper between her thumb and index finger, gave it a little shake, and plunk! The number 189 fell out onto the desk, from where it jumped to the ground and ran around, hobbling joyously, and finally ran out by the door, which the Holy Virgin had left open. And nobody was surprised, for you get all sorts in Paradise: people, animals, objects... even numbers!

"You have passed our entrance exams," said the Virgin Mary. "Now, come with me."

And she took the little devil with her, first of all to the showers, in order to wash away a few little sins he might still have behind his ears. Then to the clothes depot, where he exchanged his bat-wings for a beautiful pair of swan's wings. Lastly to the hairdresser, who tried to saw his horns off. But they were too tough, so he made do with setting a brand new, milk-white halo on top of them.

After this, they went back into the courtyard. This time it was crowded, for it was playtime, and the Mother of God introduced the little devil to the other angels.

"Here is a new companion for you," she said. "He deserves all our respect for reaching us here, for he comes from far away! Please treat him like one of the family."

There was a murmur of surprise, and one old, pink angel stepped forward:

"Excuse me, Holy Virgin, but this can't be right! An angel that is red from head to foot, with a pair of horns? Why, this is unheard of!"

"You are a bunch of ninnies, aren't you?" said the Virgin Mary. "True: you've never seen a red angel before. So what? Is this the very first time you are seeing something you have never seen before?"

The other angels burst out laughing and the aged pink angel politely admitted that his comment had been silly.

Now the little devil lives in heaven. And if Paradise

were not Paradise, the other angels would be envious of his fine red skin and his black horns.

As for his devil father, when he learnt what had happened, he shook his head:

"I might have bet this would happen," he said. "It had to end like this. Thanks to his hopeless, devil-may-care attitude, our son has finished up in God's hands! Well, it's just too bad! Let me never hear his name again!"

Now, if ever you take a holiday in Hell, you must take care not to mention the tale of the good little devil. Down there, his story is considered a very bad example for the young ones, and their parents will soon find a way to make you be quiet!

The Love Story of a Potato

There was once a potato—a common potato, such as we see every day—but this one was eaten up with ambition. Her lifelong dream was to become a French fry. And this is probably what would have happened to her, had the youngest boy in the house not stolen her from the kitchen.

As soon as he had his booty safely in his bedroom, the little boy pulled a knife from his pocket and set about carving the potato. He began by giving her two eyes—and at once the potato could see. After which he gave her two ears—and the potato was able to hear. Finally, he gave her a mouth—and the potato was able to speak. Then the boy made her look at herself in a mirror, saying:

"See how beautiful you are!"

"How dreadful!" replied the potato. "I am not

the least bit beautiful. I look like a boy! I was much happier before."

"Fine, okay then!" replied the little boy, annoyed. "If that's how you see it..."

And he threw the potato in the bin.

Early the next morning, the bin was emptied and, later that day, the potato was dumped along with a great heap of other rubbish, in the middle of the countryside.

"An attractive region," she said, "and very popular at that! What a collection of fascinating people there are here... Now, who can that be, looking rather like a frying pan?"

It was an old guitar, nearly split in half, with only two strings left intact.

"Hello there, madame," said the potato. "It seems to me, from your appearance, that you must be a very distinguished person, for you bear a marvellous resemblance to a frying pan!"

"You are very kind," said the guitar. "I do not know what a frying pan would be, but I thank you all the same. It's true that I'm not just anybody. My name is Guitar. And yours?"

"Well, my name is Maris Piper. But you can call me

Potato for, from today, I shall count you an intimate friend. Because of my beauty, I was selected to become a French fry, and I should have become one had I not suffered the misfortune of being stolen from the kitchen by the youngest boy in the house. What is worse, having stolen me, the scoundrel completely disfigured me with these pairs of eyes and ears and this awful mouth..."

And the potato began to cry.

"Now, now, don't cry," said the guitar. "You are still very elegant. And besides, this means you can speak..."

"That's true," agreed the potato. "It's a great consolation. In the end—to finish my story—when I saw what that little monster had done to me, I was furious, and I wrenched the knife right out of his hands, cut off his nose and ran away."

"Well done, you!" the guitar responded.

"Don't you think?" said the potato. "But, what about you? How do you come to be here?"

"Well," replied the guitar, "for many years I was best friends with a handsome young boy, who loved me dearly. He used to bend over me, take me in his arms, caress me, strum me, pluck the strings on my belly while singing such delightful songs to me..."

The guitar sighed, then her voice grew bitter and she went on:

"One day he came back with a strange instrument. This one was also a guitar, but made of metal, and oh so heavy, vulgar and stupid! She took my friend from me, she bewitched him. I am sure he didn't really love her. He never sang her any tender songs when he picked her up—not one! He used to pluck furiously at her strings and give savage howls and roll about on the ground with her—you would have thought they were fighting! Besides, he didn't trust her! The plain proof is that he kept her tied up on a leash!"

In fact, what had happened was that the handsome young man had bought an electric guitar, and what our guitar had taken for a leash was in fact the wire that connected the new guitar to the electricity.

"Anyway, however it happened, she stole him from me. After only a few days he only had eyes for her, he no longer looked at me at all. And when I saw that, well, I preferred to leave him..."

The guitar was lying. She had not left of her own accord; her master had thrown her out. But she would never have admitted that.

In any case, the potato hadn't understood a word.

"What a beautiful story!" she said. "How moving! I'm quite beside myself. I knew we were made to understand each other. Besides, the more I look at you, the more I feel you look like a frying pan!"

But while they were chatting like this, a tramp going by on the high road heard them, stopped and listened harder.

"Now this is no ordinary how-d'ye-do," he thought. "An old guitar telling her life story to an old potato, and the potato answering. If I can do this right, I'll be a rich man!"

He found a way into the wasteland, picked up the potato and put her in his pocket, then he grabbed the guitar and took the two friends with him to the next town.

This town had a large central square, and in the square there was a circus. The tramp went and knocked on the circus ringmaster's door.

"Mista Ringmaster! Mista Ringmaster sir!"

"Hmph? What? Come in! What do you want?"

The tramp stepped into the caravan.

"Mista Ringmaster, I have a talking guitar!"

"Hmph? What? Talking guitar?"

"Yes yes, Mista Ringmaster! And a potato that answers it back!"

"Hmph? What? What is this story? Are you drunk, my friend?"

"No, no, I'm not drunk. Please just listen!"

The tramp put the guitar on the table, then took the potato from his pocket and put them next to each other.

"Now, hop to it. Talk, you two!"

Silence.

"Talk, I tell you!"

More silence. The Ringmaster's face flushed an angry red.

"Tell me, my friend, did you come here purely to make a fool of me?"

"Of course not, Mista Ringmaster! I'm telling you, they do talk, both of them, to each other. Just now, they're being difficult so as to annoy me, but..."

"Get out!"

"But when they are alone..."

"I said: get out!"

"But Mista Ringmaster..."

"Hm? What? You haven't left yet? Very good, I shall throw you out myself!"

The ringmaster caught the tramp by the seat of his pants and—therr-whumpp!—he tossed him out. But at that very moment, he heard a great burst of laughter behind him. Unable to hold her tongue any longer, the potato had just said to the guitar:

"Hey, do you think we fooled him? He he he!"

"And how! We fooled him good and proper!" the guitar was saying. "Ha ha ha!"

The ringmaster whirled around:

"Well I never, how about that! The old drunk was telling the truth. You can talk, both of you!"

Silence.

"Come on," the ringmaster went on. "There's no point keeping quiet now. You can't fool me any longer: I heard you!"

Silence.

"That is a pity!" the ringmaster said then, with a cunning expression. "I had a rather exciting proposal for you. An artistic proposal!"

"Artistic?" asked the guitar.

"Shut up!" hissed the potato.

"But I adore art!"

"Now we're getting somewhere!" said the ringmaster. "I can see that you're a sensible pair.

And indeed, you will have work, both of you—oh yes you will. You will become stars."

"I'd rather become a French fry," objected the potato.

"A French fry? You—with your talent? That would be a crime! Would you really prefer to be eaten than to be famous?"

"What do you mean, 'eaten'? Do people eat French fries?" asked the potato.

"Do we *eat* French fries? Of course we eat them! Why do you think we're always frying more?"

"Really? I didn't know!" said the potato. "Well, if that's how things stand, then fine. I'd rather become a star."

A week later, all over the town, big yellow posters appeared on which were written:

THE FABULOUS CIRCUS OF WHATSIT

See clowns! See acrobats!
Bareback riders! Trapeze-artists!
See tigers, ponies, elephants, fleas!
And, in their world premiere show:
NOÉMIE, the performing potato
And AGATHE, the guitar who plays herself!

The big top was full on the new show's first night, for nobody in that part of the world had seen anything like it before.

When their turn came, the band played a military march while the potato and the guitar stepped bravely into the ring. To start with, the potato introduced their number. Then the guitar played a difficult piece by herself. Then the potato sang a song, accompanied by the guitar, who sang a harmony while playing herself at the same time. And then, the potato pretended to sing a wrong note and the guitar pretended to catch her out. The potato pretended to get angry and they both pretended to have a big argument, to the great delight of the audience. Finally, they pretended to make up and be friends again and they sang their last song together.

The potato and the guitar were a huge success. Their act was recorded for radio and for television and, soon, people were talking about it all over the world. Having seen it on the news, the Sultan of Bakofbiyondistan flew over that afternoon in his private jet, to see the ringmaster.

"Hello, Mister Ringmaster."

"Hello, Mister Sultan. What can I do for you?"

"I should like to marry the potato."

"The potato? Now, look here, she's not a person!"

"Very well, I'll buy her."

"But she's not an object either... She speaks, she can sing..."

"Very well, I'll take her from you!"

"But you've no right to do that!"

"It's my right to do anything I please, for I have oodles of money!"

The ringmaster realized he should try to be a little cleverer.

"You will cause me great sadness," he said, sobbing. "I love that potato, I've grown attached to her..."

"And how I sympathize!" said the Sultan, with just a hint of sarcasm. "In that case, I can offer you a caravan full of diamonds for her!"

"Just the one caravan?" asked the ringmaster.

"Two, if you prefer!"

The ringmaster wiped away a tear, blew his nose loudly, then added in a wobbly voice:

"I feel, if you were to go as far as three caravans..."

"Done! Three it shall be, and let that be an end of it."

The next day, the Sultan flew back to his sultanate, taking the potato with him, and also the guitar, for the two old friends were determined to stay together. That week, a popular weekly magazine published a photograph of the brand-new couple with the following front-page headline:

WE LOVE EACH OTHER

In the weeks that followed, the same magazine published more photos, and the headlines changed accordingly. In order of appearance, they went like this:

WILL THE GOVERNMENT DARE TO STOP THEM?

WILL IT BREAK THE POTATO'S HEART?

POTATO SAYS, WEEPING: THIS CAN'T GO ON!

GUITAR SAYS: I'D RATHER GO!

AND STILL THEY ARE IN LOVE!

LOVE CONQUERS ALL

And beneath that last headline followed more photographs—from the wedding of the Sultan and the potato. Only a week later, the newspapers were full of other news, and soon, everyone had forgotten all about the love story of the Sultan, the potato and the guitar.

Uncle Pierre's House

In a village in France there lived two brothers, one who was rich while the other was poor. The rich brother was a bachelor; the poor one was married. The rich one had plenty of money and did not need to work, while the poor one was a farm worker. The poor one had no house of his own; instead he and his wife lived in the house of the farmer who employed him, while the rich brother had a big house, less than a mile from the village, after the graveyard.

The poor brother was friendly with everyone, and only wanted to be helpful. Consequently, all the local people liked him, although they also looked down on him a little. The rich brother, however, was greedy, a mean and dour type, so that, while they respected him a lot, the people did not like him much.

*

177

One fine morning, the farmer who employed the poor brother said to him:

"Look, autumn is almost over, the main tasks are done and I can't afford to pay you to do nothing. Take your wife and be off with you."

What could he do? Where could he go? The poor man and his wife went to see his rich brother.

"The farmer has sent us away," he said, "and we haven't even a place to live during the winter. Could you perhaps put us up? Only until the spring?"

The rich man frowned. He enjoyed being alone and undisturbed in his big house. However, he could not leave his brother out in the cold. He replied:

"Well, of course, come in and make yourselves at home. You can sleep in the upstairs bedroom and I'll take the big room downstairs. But take note, it's on one condition!"

"What's that?"

"That you will never go out in the evening after dinner, and that you will be in bed by nine o'clock at the latest!"

"Of course!" said the poor man.

That day, he and his wife moved into the upstairs bedroom.

For three months, that's how they lived. The poor brother's wife did the cooking and, during the day, the poor brother himself criss-crossed the village looking for odd jobs. Meanwhile, the rich brother did nothing; he was always deep in thought. They had their meals together and, after dinner, as soon as the table was cleared, the poor brother and his wife said goodnight to the rich brother and went up to bed. The rich man stayed up very late in the big room on the ground floor, where his oil lamp glimmered long into the night.

"What can he be doing, up so late, all by himself?" wondered the poor man's wife.

And the poor man answered:

"He can do whatever he likes; it is his house."

But his wife wanted to find out. One fine evening, on the stroke of eleven, she softly went back down the stairs, barefoot and in the pitch dark. The door to the downstairs room was ajar. Silently, she tiptoed towards it and peeked inside: there she saw her brother-in-law sitting at the great dining table, taking gold coins one by one out of a little iron box and stacking them in tall piles.

She went back upstairs and said to her husband:

"I know what your brother is doing."

"What is he doing?"

"He's counting gold."

"And why not? It's his gold, after all."

December went by, and January too. One bright morning towards the middle of February, the poor man's wife came downstairs to light the fire and make the coffee. The rich man was still asleep in bed. She went over to wake him and saw that he had died, and it must have been quite suddenly, during the night.

Hearing this, the poor brother was genuinely upset. The two brothers had loved and respected each other, despite their different personalities.

That morning, the couple went to see a lawyer. Since he had no children, all the rich man's belongings would go to the poor man, who was, therefore, no longer poor.

That same afternoon, the husband and wife looked through every room in the house very carefully. They found some money in cash and some more in bonds—enough to guarantee them a good living to the end of their days.

But the wife was not satisfied:

"There is gold hidden in this house," she said. "I'm certain of it. I've seen it."

They rummaged through everything again, from the cellar to the attic, without finding either the gold or the little iron box.

"Perhaps you dreamt it," her husband suggested.

"I'm quite sure I did not," replied his wife. "I saw gold, real gold coins, in a little iron box, like a biscuit tin. But he's hidden it well!"

"Too bad, then," said her husband. "Besides, we've no need of it now. We have quite enough money to live on."

The funeral was held the following morning and, that evening, for the first time, instead of going to bed, the husband and wife stayed up after dinner in the big room on the ground floor.

When midnight struck, they were still there. Hardly had the twelve strokes rung out from the village church than they heard behind them a rough voice:

"Well, well, what are you two doing here?"

They span around: it was the rich brother, or rather his ghost, dressed just as he had been when alive.

"Is that you, Pierre?" asked the poor brother.

The ghost continued without answering him:

"I thought I told you that you must be in bed every evening by nine o'clock..."

"But now that you are dead..." protested the poor brother.

"*What* are you saying?" thundered the ghost in a terrible voice.

"I'm saying that you are dead!"

"And what do you mean by *that*?"

"We mean that you are dead!" said the wife, brusquely. "Now, don't you remember? We only buried you this morning!"

At this, the ghost got really angry:

"What on earth is this nonsense? A fabrication, so as to steal what's rightfully mine from under my nose, is that it? Is this the thanks I get for taking you into my home? And you expect me to believe this codswallop? Get off to bed with you, this minute!"

Shamefaced, the couple went back up to their old bedroom. The husband got undressed and into bed, then said to his wife:

"What's up? Aren't you coming to bed?"

His wife replied:

"I still want to see what he's up to."

"Don't go," said her husband. "It's not wise."

The wife shrugged.

"Why not? What do you think he'll do to me?"

Down she went, as she had the first time, barefoot and in the dark, and peering through the half-open door, just like the first time, she saw her brother-in-law sitting at the great table, counting out his gold coins. But this time the ghost guessed she was there. Hardly had she seen him when he turned towards the door and shouted:

"Now what is it?"

Terrified, the wife leapt back up the stairs, four at a time.

"What is he doing?" asked her husband.

"He is still counting his money," she said.

The next day, they went to the village priest, to ask him what all this could mean. The priest listened to their story most attentively, then said:

"It is rare, but this does sometimes happen. A great passion, whether for good or for bad, can prevent a soul from being at peace. Your brother loved his gold

too much. This is why his ghost returns, every night, to count it over and over..."

"But he is dead!"

"He is indeed dead, but he hasn't accepted his death. He doesn't want to admit it has happened. However hard you argue with him, he will refuse to see the truth. His greed is keeping him here on earth. It's a great hardship; we should feel sorry for him!"

"So there's nothing to be done?"

"There's nothing to be done. This will go on until the day when he himself recognizes the absurdity of his behaviour. On that day, he will be free. But it might take centuries!"

The couple did not ask again. In any case they couldn't complain, for they had the dead man's cash and his bonds. They bought a few meadows and a small house in town, where they set up home, and there they lived, wanting for nothing, the husband working the land and his wife looking after everything indoors.

That spring, they had a little boy and, the following year, a little girl. The two children grew up and began to walk and talk. After five or six years they started attending school. Every Sunday afternoon, the two children would go for a walk together. Every time, their mother would warn them:

"Do not stray anywhere near the graveyard, and above all never go into your Uncle Pierre's house. He'll be very angry."

She didn't say any more, for she did not want to frighten them needlessly.

However, one fine spring evening, the children were caught out in a thunderstorm just as they happened to be walking on the far side of the graveyard. It began to rain heavily, and soon very heavily, there were flashes of lightning and it didn't look like stopping soon, for the light had turned a hazy grey and the sky was black all over.

"Let's take shelter in that house," said the little girl.

The little boy recognized Uncle Pierre's house and he hesitated for a moment. Then he decided that the village was still a while away, that his little sister might be taken ill and that, however unwelcoming Uncle Pierre might be, he could not refuse them shelter.

They stepped straight into the main room. There they found a bed that seemed not to have been made for years. They took off their wet clothes, hung them out on the backs of the chairs, then lay down nice and dry and went to sleep.

Unawares, the children slept deeply for several hours, until they were awoken by a grumpy voice:

"What are you doing here?"

"Excuse us, monsieur," said the little boy. "We were just looking for somewhere to shelter. We didn't mean to stay. We fell asleep…"

"So I see: you did indeed fall asleep. First, who are you? What are your names?"

The little boy told him his name, his sister's name and their surname. The ghost raised his eyebrows.

"So that's how it is: you are my niece and nephew?"

"Yes, Uncle."

"Now I understand! My brother has sent you here—to spy on me. Perhaps to steal from me!"

"You're mistaken, Uncle, I assure you! On the contrary, our parents told us never to enter your house! It's all my fault!"

"Your parents told you, your parents told you… And why would they tell you such a thing, anyway? Am I some kind of ogre?"

"Umm… so we wouldn't disturb you, surely…"

"Enough nonsense! I know why they told you to

keep away—to make you afraid of me! There! They want people to think I'm dead, so they can get my gold... What gold, anyway! There's no gold here. And what would I be doing with gold?

"Anyway, I'm not dead! Not at all! As long as I'm here, they shan't have a single gold sovereign of it! Besides, there's no gold here. I haven't any. There's nothing here but these four walls, that's all. You can tell your father that from me. Got it?"

"Yes, Uncle..."

"Right, then what are you waiting for? Get dressed and scarper, both of you!"

The two children had not understood a word of this flood of speech, but they got dressed and were just leaving when the ghost stopped them:

"Now where are you off to? You can see it's still raining. Stay here! And take those clothes off— they're still quite sodden. They'll go about saying I'm heartless all over again! That's right, hang them out by the fire."

"But there is no fire!" the little boy pointed out.

"No fire? What's that, then?"

The ghost waved his hand and a roaring fire appeared in the fireplace.

"Each of you take a blanket. Sit yourselves near and warm those feet. Now you have distracted me, I shan't be able to work any more tonight. I will come and warm myself beside you. An evening wasted thanks to you!"

"Forgive us, Uncle..."

"Be quiet. Did I ask you anything? Oh, I know, I know: there are plenty besides the four of you who would like to know... But they won't find out a thing! What did you think? That I would show you my little secrets? Your old uncle's not quite the fool you take him for! And anyway, I have no secrets... There's nothing here but these four walls, and that's all. No more than that... No more..."

All three were sitting around the fire, the two children wrapped in blankets and the old man muttering softly away, more for his own benefit than for theirs. In a few minutes, grown drowsy from the fire's heat, lulled by Uncle Pierre's gentle drone and helped along by the lateness of the hour, the little boy dropped off to sleep in his chair.

A burst of laughter woke him up. His little sister was giggling helplessly. The little boy's eyes flew open and he saw something incredible: Uncle

Pierre had himself fallen asleep, and the little girl had tried to climb into his lap. She had got up, gone over to the armchair and, passing right through the ghost's ethereal body, she had found herself sitting right *inside* Uncle Pierre's tummy, which is what had made her giggle.

Now the little boy was really afraid. Not at seeing that Uncle Pierre was not really all there—if that's how things were, then that's how things were, he felt—but he was afraid that their uncle might get angry, that he might find the little girl's behaviour disrespectful.

"Please forgive her," he said, "she only wanted to play..."

But Uncle Pierre was not listening. Having himself only just jolted awake, he too was staring down in shock at the little girl sitting inside his stomach, giggling away and rocking back and forth, wiggling her two little bare feet in the air.

"So it was true," he muttered, "so it was true after all..."

Then his eye fell on the little boy and he asked gravely:

"Do you also find this funny?"

"No, Uncle."

"Does it frighten you, then?"

"No, Uncle."

Uncle Pierre narrowed his lips, then he gave a mean smile and asked one more question:

"Do you know what a ghost is?"

"No, Uncle."

There was a silence. The little girl had stopped laughing; the ghost seemed to be thinking. Then he stood up and said:

"Wait for me here, I'll be back soon."

He went out. Just then, the little girl, who was still sitting there, found herself alone in the chair, took fright and began to cry. The boy took her to sit on his lap. Five minutes later, the ghost was back with a small iron box which he set down on the table.

"Give this to your parents tomorrow morning. And now, go to bed. Goodbye."

The children went back to bed and were asleep as soon as their heads touched the pillows. When they awoke the next day, it was broad daylight and Uncle Pierre had vanished. Their clothes had dried out during the night so they put them back on and went home, carrying with them the little iron box full of gold coins.

There are people in that part of the world who claim that the little box never existed and that the children had merely dreamt a wild dream that night. I have not been able to check whether the little box did exist. But one thing is for certain, that since that day Uncle Pierre's ghost was never seen again in the old house, or anywhere else.

Prince Blub and the Mermaid

T here was once an old king whose kingdom was an island, a magnificent island in the midst of the tropics, right in the middle of the ocean.

This king had a young son whose name was Prince Henri Marie François Guy Pierre Antoine. A very long name for such a small prince! So long that, when he was little, every time someone asked him:

"What is your name?"

He generally replied:

"Blub."

So everybody ended up calling him Prince Blub.

They don't have winter in the tropics. So, instead of washing in the bathroom every morning, which is dreadfully boring, Prince Blub would go and bathe in the sea. He had his own little beach among the rocks, all to himself, only five minutes from the palace. And every day he would meet a mermaid there and they would play together, as they had done ever since he was a baby.

You know, don't you, what a mermaid is. It is a sea creature that is half woman and half fish: her top half is a woman, while the rest of her is simply a long fishtail.

The mermaid would lift Blub onto her shoulders and carry him right around the island. Or she would swim with him out on the high seas. Or she might take him diving for shells, tiny fish, crabs and sticks of coral. When they were tired of swimming together, they would stretch out on the rocks and the mermaid would tell tales about all the wonders of the ocean while Prince Blub dried off in the sun.

One day when they were chatting like this, Prince Blub said to the mermaid:

"When I'm grown up, I shall marry you."

The mermaid smiled.

"When you're grown up," she said, "you'll marry a beautiful princess, who will have two legs like all of you humans, not an ugly fishtail, and one day you will be king just like your father."

"No," insisted the Prince. "I only want to marry *you*."

"You're not allowed to decide," replied the mermaid. "You don't know what you're saying. When you're fifteen years old, we'll talk about it properly."

Prince Blub did not complain.

Years passed and he grew up into a handsome young man. One day, he said to the mermaid:

"Don't you know what's happening to me today?"

"What?"

"I'm turning fifteen."

"So what?"

"So what? Well, I still love you and I would like to marry you."

This time the mermaid grew thoughtful.

"Listen Blub," she said, "I believe you mean it, but you don't know what you're talking about. You can see that I have no legs: therefore, I can't live on earth with you like a normal woman. If you marry me, it is you who will have to follow *me* to my father's house, in the Kingdom of Under-Water. You will become a water sprite and have to exchange your two lovely legs for the tail of a fish..."

"But that would be fine!" he exclaimed.

"No it wouldn't be fine," she retorted. "You are not the first man to want to marry a mermaid, you know! Yet these marriages are always unhappy. First, in the majority of cases, the men marry us for their own advantage. They marry us so as to live for ever, for water sprites are immortal..."

"But," said Prince Blub, "I didn't know that..."

"I know, I know, but let me finish. Then, once they're married, they start missing life on earth, missing their two legs and the land where they grew up. They want to be able to jump and run once more; they think about flowers, butterflies, animals, the old friends they have left behind... they get bored to death, and yet they know that they will never die..."

"But I love you," said the Prince, "and I'm sure I won't regret anything."

The mermaid shook her head.

"You haven't a clue. When you are twenty, we'll talk about it again."

But this time, the Prince did not want to wait. That very day, over lunch, he said to his father the King:

"You know, Papa, I am going to marry a mermaid."

"Don't be stupid," said the King. "You know very well that mermaids do not exist."

"I beg your pardon," said the Prince, "but I'm friends with one. I go swimming with her every morning."

The King did not reply, but when he had finished his coffee, he went to see the Royal Chaplain.

"Tell me, Father, is it true that mermaids exist?"

"Alas, yes, they do exist," replied the Chaplain. "And in fact they are demons!"

"What do you mean, they are demons?"

"Well, you see: mermaids are the female kind of water sprite. And water sprites are immortal. Since they are immortal, they never die. Since they do not die, they never go to heaven. Since they never go to heaven, they never encounter God. As a result, they must be sad creatures indeed... But they are not sad; on the contrary! They are as gay as starlings—therefore they must be demons! Their very existence is an insult to our Good Lord. Do you understand?"

"Yes, yes..." muttered the King.

He went to find his son.

"You did tell me you're in love with a mermaid, didn't you?"

"Yes, Father."

"And you want to marry her?"

"Yes, Father."

"You have no idea, then, that mermaids are demons?"

"That's not true!" replied Prince Blub, indignantly. "Someone's told you wrong. My mermaid is not a demon. She is as sweet and kind as anyone!"

"Yes, yes..." answered the King, very puzzled.

He went back to find the Chaplain.

"Hm. Look here, Father... When we spoke, I wasn't sure how to tell you... but my son has fallen in love with a mermaid."

"This is a disaster!" screeched the Chaplain. "First, if your son marries her, he won't go to heaven. And then, he will become a water sprite and, instead of legs, he will have nothing but a fishtail. Lastly, he will be obliged to live in the sea for evermore, and will never be able to become king after you..."

"But this is indeed a disaster!" cried the King, horrified. "What shall I do?"

"Tell him that mermaids are demons..."

"I have already told him but he won't believe me."

"In that case, they must be separated. No matter what it takes!"

"That," said the King, "is a good idea. I shall think about it."

For the second time, he went to speak to the Prince.

"You did tell me that you're in love with a mermaid, didn't you?"

"Yes, Father."

"Do you still wish to marry her?"

"Yes, Father."

"Are you quite sure you won't regret it?"

"I shall never regret it!" exclaimed the Prince. "I will live with her in the ocean and we will be perfectly happy!"

"Yes, yes... Well, in that case... When will you see this mermaid again?"

"Tomorrow morning, Father, on the beach."

"Right, then," he said. "Tell her that, the day after tomorrow, I will come with you. I would like to meet her."

The following morning, standing at the water's edge, the Prince told the mermaid:

"My father is happy for me to marry you! Tomorrow morning he will come with me to meet you!"

The mermaid laughed:

"Your father is clever, for this is all a trap! But never mind: let him come and I will be here. As for you, don't be afraid, for, whatever happens, I am immortal. And even if we are parted, I shall tell you how to find me again."

"How?" asked the Prince.

"Pay attention: when you want to see me, find a place where there is water—however little, as long as there is some..."

"Even if it is not connected to the sea?"

"Even if it is not connected to the sea. I am at home everywhere there is water. For all the waters of the world are only one and the same water, and my father rules them all. To make me appear, you have only to be near water—no need even to touch it—and to sing this little song:

> *One and one make one*
> *Mermaid my wife to be*
> *I am your dearest water sprite*
> *And you will spend your life with me*

That morning, Prince Blub sang the song over several times in a row so that, by the time he was home, he knew it by heart.

The next day, the King came to the beach with his son, accompanied by a large retinue of courtiers.

What the Prince did not know was that these courtiers were in fact mostly policemen, fish merchants and fishermen, dressed up as courtiers, with ropes, fishing line, clubs and revolvers hidden beneath their fine court clothes.

The mermaid was waiting for them, sitting on a rock. The King approached her, took her by the wrist as if to kiss her hand, then yelled to everyone in his retinue:

"Go!"

At this signal, they all jumped on the mermaid and trapped her in their nets, pinned her down and finished by tying her up. When he tried to defend her, Prince Blub was attacked too, and tied up and gagged, before he could do a single thing.

This done, the King told his fishermen:

"Take this monster away and cut her tail into pieces to sell at the market."

Then, turning to Prince Blub, he added:

"And as for you, my very dear son, I am sending you on the next plane to see my cousin the Emperor of Russia, who will keep you with him until you have given up this ridiculous notion of being in love!"

*

That very afternoon, Prince Blub flew to Moscow, while the mermaid, still tied up, was left lying on a metal counter in one of the capital's great fishmonger's.

There she lay, calmly, saying not a word in protest and smiling serenely. The fishmonger went up to her with a long knife, yet she kept on smiling. He cut off her tail, took it away and laid it on another counter, then came back. To his great surprise, he saw that her tail had grown back and that, instead of being pink and white, the mermaid had turned green—green from head to foot, including her hair—while her smile had become fixed in a slightly disturbing grin.

Uneasy, the fishmonger chopped off the second tail, the green one, and took it over to the other counter, to lay it beside the pink tail. Then he hurried back, as quickly as he could, and... this time the mermaid had turned sky-blue, from the locks of her bright blue hair to the tip of her brand-new blue tail! What's more, she was no longer really smiling at all, but grimacing horribly.

Trembling with fear, the fishmonger attempted the operation once more. But as soon as he cut off the third tail and set it down beside the first two, the mermaid became quite black; her tail now black; scales all black;

skin, hair and face quite black; and her grimace had grown so furious, so frighteningly ugly that the poor, terrified man backed out of his shop and, tossing his knife away, raced all the way to the palace without stopping, to tell the King what had happened.

Deeply intrigued, the King wanted to go back to the fishmonger's with him to see what they would find. But when they got there, the mermaid had vanished completely and, likewise, vanished too were the pink tail, the green tail and even the blue one.

Meanwhile, Prince Blub had been welcomed by the Emperor of Russia. The Emperor had given Blub rooms in a private apartment in the Kremlin, where the Emperor's servants could spy on him.

As soon as he thought he was alone, the Prince went into the bathroom, ran a bath and, when the tub was full, began to sing:

> *One and one make one*
> *Mermaid my wife to be*
> *I am your dearest water sprite*
> *And you will spend your life with me*

Then the water bubbled up and the mermaid appeared.

"Hello Prince Blub. Do you love me?"

"Yes I do love you. I want to marry you."

"You must wait a bit; our test has begun."

With these words, she dived into the water and disappeared.

But one of the servants had seen everything through the keyhole. He went straight away to make a report to the Emperor, and the Emperor informed Prince Blub that from now on the bathroom was out of bounds.

The following day, the Prince called for a basin of water to wash his hands. It was brought to him. He took it, with thanks, put it down on the floor in the middle of his room and began to sing:

One and one make one
Mermaid my wife to be
I am your dearest water sprite
And you will spend your life with me

And then the water bubbled up and the mermaid appeared—although just a little smaller, for the basin was narrower than the bathtub.

"Hello Prince Blub. Do you still love me?"

"I love you, I adore you."

"Keep waiting, then, for our test is under way."

And with these words, she dived into the water and disappeared.

That day, the Emperor informed Prince Blub that from now on he was banned from doing any washing at all.

Now the Prince realized that all the servants were no better than spies.

On the third day, he pretended to be thirsty and called for a glass of water. His valet brought one. The Prince took the glass and set it on a table, then, instead of sending the valet away, he said:

"Sit here. And watch."

Now, himself sitting down in front of the glass, he began to sing:

> *One and one make one*
> *Mermaid my wife to be*
> *I am your dearest water sprite*
> *And you will spend your life with me*

At this, the water fizzed and popped and there was the mermaid: very tiny, miniature even, but quite recognizable.

"Hello Prince Blub. Do you still love me?"

"Yes I love you. I want to marry you."

"Wait just a little longer; our test is over."

With these words, the mermaid dived down inside the glass, where she appeared to dissolve within a second.

Now Prince Blub picked up the glass and threw all the water in the valet's face, saying:

"Now, you nosy telltale, go and do your low-down job."

We must imagine that the valet did go and tell his tale, for, the following morning, the Emperor sent Prince Blub back to his father, along with the following note:

My dear cousin,

I have done what I could, but it is impossible to stop your son from calling up the mermaid, short of making him die of thirst. I am sending him back, and pray God keep you all safe.

Signed NIKITA the Great
Emperor of Russia

The King read this letter, then went back to the Royal Chaplain, again.

"The Emperor has sent my son back," he explained, "and this is what he wrote to me."

"If this is how it is," replied the Chaplain, "I see only one solution: turn the Prince into a postage stamp and stick him to the wall, in the driest part of the palace, so that not a drop of water will touch him!"

"Now that," said the King, "is a good idea! Don't move a muscle, I'll send him to you right away."

He went to fetch his son and asked him, in an offhand manner:

"Tell me, my boy, would you like to do something nice for your father?"

"Of course!" said Prince Blub.

"Well then, go fetch me the Chaplain. I need to speak to him."

Prince Blub went to the Chaplain's rooms and knocked on the door.

"Who is there?" called the Chaplain.

"It's Prince Blub."

"Come in!"

The Prince stepped inside and, the second he opened his mouth to say "My father wants you", the Chaplain, staring at him, began very rapidly and without stumbling to recite:

Abracadabra
Flatter and flatter
*Abracadab*rea
As small as a flea
*Abracadab*rare
A small paper square
*Abracad*brick
To lick
And to stick
You young
Disobedient one!

By the last line, the Prince had become a postage stamp and was fluttering down onto the floor. The chaplain picked him up and took him to the king.

He was a very handsome stamp, in three colours and with bevelled edges framing a portrait of the Prince, and bearing the following inscription:

ROYAL MAIL, 30 PENCE

The king eyed it closely and asked:

"Do you still wish to marry your mermaid?"

A tiny voice emerged from the stamp, squeaking:

"Yes, I still want to!"

"In that case," the King warned, "I shall stick you on the wall and you will stay there until you change your mind."

But just as he was preparing to lick the stamp, the Chaplain cried out:

"No, no, not that! Don't wet it!"

"True, true," the King acknowledged. "Saliva has water in it too!"

So he took a pot of white glue and, using a fine paintbrush, stuck the stamp to the wall above his desk.

Days, weeks and months went by. Every morning, before he started work, the king would look up at the stamp and ask:

"Do you still want to marry your mermaid?"

And the little voice would reply:

"Yes, I still want to."

It rained a lot that year. There were downpours, storms and tempests. There was even a whirlwind that rose out of the sea and swept through the island from one end to the other. But the royal palace was well built and not one drop of water reached the King's study.

The next year it did not rain much but there was

an earthquake, followed by a tidal wave. One section of the island broke away and the entire coastline was flooded. But the King's palace was solid and set high on a cliff, so that not a single drop of water could reach the postage stamp.

And then, the following year, there was a war. One fine day, the President of the Republic of a neighbouring island sent a dozen aeroplanes to bomb the royal palace.

The King, the Queen and their entire court had time to go down to the cellar, but when they came back up, the palace was on fire.

Seeing the flames, the King panicked. He loved his son dearly, although he was hard on him, and he would rather have let him marry the mermaid than leave him to burn. While his men made a human chain, passing up buckets of water, the King went back into the burning palace, a glass of water in his hand, ready to risk his life. Flames were dancing everywhere; the smoke was blinding and made him cough, and sparks were flying like cannonballs; the King's royal cloak was getting singed at the edges. By a great stroke of luck, the royal study was still untouched by the flames and the bombs. The King searched the walls for the Prince's stamp, found it and kissed it, weeping:

"Be happy, my son, be happy," he murmured.

Then he tried to throw his glassful of water over the stamp... but the stamp had disappeared. One of the King's tears had moistened it when he was kissing it and this was enough: Prince Blub had gone to join the mermaids' kingdom.

Almost instantly, rain began to pour down in torrents and soon the fire was under control. Half an hour later, the King was discovered in a deep faint, lying on the floor of his office, with a broken glass in his right hand.

He was helped up, carried away and set to rights, but hardly had he started to feel better than he received terrible news: the enemy fleet had been sighted. It was approaching at top speed and would try to land an army on the island.

The King called his advisers together and sent out all his battleships. He had little hope, for the enemy soldiers were more numerous, better armed and better trained. After giving some orders and doing everything he personally could, the King went for a walk by himself, at the water's edge, on the very beach where the young Prince Blub had gone swimming with the mermaid. As he walked, the King grieved and wept:

"Oh my son, my child, in what terrible straits you leave your land!"

Hardly had he said this than Prince Blub was there before him, riding among the wavelets. He was completely naked, but still entirely decent for, below the waist, his body was nothing but the tail of a fish. Seeing his son transformed, the old King began to cry even harder, unable to say another word.

"Don't weep, Father," said Blub the water sprite, in a gentle voice. "You saved my life, you managed to choose my happiness over your anger; now be reassured: you will not regret it. For now I am one of the princes of the sea and I shall protect you. Look at the horizon!"

The old King obeyed, and trembled where he stood, for the first enemy ships were already visible and were speeding in towards them.

"My God!" he moaned.

"Look again," said Prince Blub.

The ships were still approaching, but now all around them the sea was frothing white and undulating strangely, then it grew blacker and blacker. Little by little, it was filling with strange things; living, moving things. Here and there could be seen the lash of a flipper, the twist of a tail, a mouth yawning open. The enemy fleet seemed to be sailing upon a sea of monsters.

"Now, attack!" called Prince Blub, softly.

And straight away the tables were turned. Tentacles flew, jaws opened, water spouts sprayed. The sea foamed and frothed and parted in every direction. A thousand sea monsters threw themselves upon the ships, snapping, chewing, gouging, twisting, breaking and tearing asunder everything that could be torn. The ships loomed and pitched, as if about capsize, then recovered, shuddered and shook, then fell back onto their sides, tilted, tipped bows first into the sea, struggled like injured animals, smashing against one another, some even rolling upon the waves like people with their clothes on fire.

Within half an hour, the sea was deserted and calm, the horizon empty and blue and the enemy fleet entirely destroyed.

"Let me introduce you to my wife," said Prince Blub.

The King looked down: there was the mermaid, pink and white once more, and the Prince had one arm round her waist.

"I... I'm so sorry," said the King, upset.

"Don't be sorry," said the mermaid, smiling.

"You are too good... So, tell me now: will you have children?"

"No," replied Prince Blub.

"Why not?"

"We are immortal," explained the mermaid. "Immortal people have no need to reproduce."

"Fair enough," said the King. "Sadly, the same is not true for me."

There was an uncomfortable silence.

"That is true," said Prince Blub to the mermaid. "My father has no heir, and he is worried that when he dies—"

"There will be chaos," the King broke in. "Chaos and war. For enemies will see their chance, as they always do!"

"If that's the only thing," said the mermaid, "I can fix everything. Tomorrow morning, let Your Majesty come and bathe at this beach, with Her Majesty the Queen. When you are in the water, you will notice a silver fish that comes to play around you. Let it play, do not be afraid of it, and within a week you will have a little boy."

So it happened. The next morning, the old King and Queen came to bathe at the same spot. A great silver fish came to play in the water around them and, a week later, they had a little baby prince.

All this happened a very long time ago. Even now, Prince Blub is happy as a water sprite. His parents are dead, of course, but their grandchildren still reign over the joyful island, and no enemy fleet ever dares to try attacking them.

The Cunning Little Pig

Once upon a time a mummy god was sitting in a big armchair, darning socks, while, sitting at the dinner table, her young god was finishing his homework.

The young god worked away in silence. And when he was finished, he asked:

"Mummy, can I be allowed to make a world?"

Mummy God looked over at him:

"Have you finished all your homework?"

"Yes, Mummy."

"Have you learnt your lessons?"

"Yes, Mummy."

"Good boy. Then, yes, you may."

"Thanks Mummy."

The young god took a piece of paper and some coloured pencils and set about making his world.

*

First, he created the sky and the earth. But the sky was empty and so was the earth, and both were covered in darkness.

So the young god created two lights: the Sun and the Moon. And he said aloud:

"Let the Sun be the man and the Moon be the lady."

So the Sun became the man and the Moon the lady, and they had a little daughter, who was called Dawn.

Next the young god made plants to grow on the earth and seaweed to grow in the sea. Then he made animals to live on the earth: some to crawl on the ground, some to swim in the sea and some to fly in the air.

Next he created people, the most intelligent of the animals to live on his earth.

When he had made all this, the earth was full of life. But in comparison, the sky looked rather empty. So the young god shouted as loudly as he could:

"Which of you animals wants to come and live in the sky?"

Everybody heard, except for the little pig, who was busy eating acorns. For the little pig is so greedy that he doesn't notice anything when he's eating.

Now all the animals that wanted to live in the sky responded to the young god's call: the ox replied, and the bull and the lion; the scorpion and the crab, whose name was Cancer; the swan and all the fish; both centaurs responded, one of them being the archer Sagittarius; both bears were there, the Little and the Great; so were the whale and the hare; the eagle and the dove; the dragon, the snake, the lynx and the giraffe all responded; there was a little girl who was called Virgo; there was a whole bunch of Greek letters, and even a few objects responded, such as Libra, the weighing scales.

This crowd of creatures came together and began to shout:

"Me! Me! Me! I want to live in the sky!"

So, the young god picked them all up, one by one, and stuck them up in the heavenly vault, with the help of those big silver drawing pins that we call stars. It did hurt them a little, but they were so happy to be living in the sky that they didn't give the star pins a second thought!

When the whole exercise was over, the sky was studded with creatures, while the stars shone in all their magnificence.

"This is all very pretty," said the Sun, "but when I rise in the morning, I'll grill them alive!"

"That's true," admitted the young god, "I hadn't thought of that!"

He pondered for a moment, then he said:

"Right, in that case, it's quite simple: every morning, young Dawn will get up before her father the Sun and take down everyone who lives in the sky. And every evening, when the Sun has set, she will pin everyone back up there!"

And this is what they did. This is why, every morning, the stars disappear, only to return again at the end of the day, after dark.

Everything being now thoroughly organized, the young god looked down on his world with satisfaction.

"You know," said Mummy God, "it's just about time for bed. You have school tomorrow!"

"I'm coming, Mummy," said the young god.

And he was about to get up when he heard a loud noise. It was the little pig racing in, as fast as he could, all out of breath and shouting as loudly as he could:

"What about me, then? What about me?"

"Well, what about you?" the young god asked.

"Why can't I go and live in the sky too?"

"Why didn't you ask me before?"

"No one told me you had to ask!"

"What do you mean, no one told you!" exclaimed the young god. "Didn't you hear, when I called for volunteers?"

"No, I didn't hear anything."

"What were you up to, that you didn't hear?"

"I think," said the little pig, blushing, "that I was eating acorns..."

"Well, hard luck for you!" said the young god. "If you weren't such a greedy guts, you might have heard me. I did shout very loudly!"

At this, the little pig began to sob:

"Oh pleeease, Mister Young God, sir! You can't leave me behind like this. Can't you squeeze me in somewhere? Tell the others to shuffle up a bit... If need be, you could pin me up on top of them! But do something, please, I don't mind kissing your feet..."

"I can't!" said the young god. "First because there's no more space, you can see that for yourself. The others can't squeeze together any closer. Besides, there aren't any more stars to pin you up there. And lastly, I haven't time: my mother has been calling me for a good minute already!"

With these words, the young god stood up from the table and went off to bed. Within ten minutes, he was asleep, and had quite forgotten about the brand-new world he had created. Meanwhile, the little pig was rolling about on the ground, sobbing:

"I want to be up in the sky! I want to live in the sky!"

But when he grew tired of rolling on the ground, he stopped and looked around, and realized the others had left him all by himself. So he settled down on the ground, laid his snout on his front trotters and began to grizzle:

"I knew they didn't like me! Nobody likes me. They all hate me—even that god! He's taken against me. He called while I was eating on purpose, so that I wouldn't hear. And he made sure to fill up the sky with everyone else double quick, so that I'd be too late. And what's that supposed to mean: that there aren't any stars left for me? Couldn't he make any more, huh? Oh, but I shall have my revenge! This isn't the end of the story! So he says there aren't any stars left for me; well, we shall see about that!"

He got up and trotted away in search of young Dawn.

Dawn had just got up, for the night was nearly over, and she was brushing her hair, getting ready to go, when the little pig trotted into her room:

"My poor little Dawn!" he said, with a sorrowful expression. "How unhappy you must be!"

"Unhappy, me? Not at all!"

"Oh, but you must be unhappy!" said the little pig. "Your parents are so hard on you!"

"Hard, my parents? Why do you say that?"

"Why? Isn't it hard to force a child of your age to get up before daylight in order to pull down all the stars in the sky? And to make her stay up until dark so as to pin them all up again? I'm shocked every time I think about it!"

"Listen," little Dawn said, "you mustn't let yourself be so easily shocked! My work is rather good fun, you know... It doesn't bother me. And besides, it isn't my parents' fault! It's the young god who ordered this!"

"Let's not even mention the young god," said the little pig, bitterly.

"Oh, I'm sorry. Have I upset you?"

"Forget it, it's nothing... You know, I only want one thing in life, and that's to serve you. But if you hate me too much to accept my offer, well then..."

"But I don't hate you!" little Dawn protested. "What is it that you want, exactly?"

"Oh, I don't want anything for myself. I simply thought to suggest..."

"Spit it out, then; what is it you'd suggest?"

The little pig lowered his voice:

"Well, if you like, I could come with you this morning and help you with your work..."

"Well," said young Dawn, "if that's all it takes to make you happy..."

"But it's not to make *me* happy!" the little pig explained, loftily. "I want to help you—that's all I want to do!"

"All right then. Let's go!"

Dawn put down her hairbrush, picked up a vast sack and slung it over her shoulder, and off they went.

As soon as they had reached the sky, they set to work. The little pig held the sack open while Dawn tossed the stars down into it pell-mell, on top of each other. As they were unpinned, the animals living up in the sky began to come down to earth where they would spend the day.

"This is wonderful!" said young Dawn. "I'm going twice as fast as usual! Thank you so much, little pig!"

"It's nothing, nothing at all!" puffed the little pig, chuckling to himself.

Now, just as Dawn was tossing the Little Bear's stars into the open sack, the little pig jumped at the most beautiful one—the Pole Star, the one that shows which way is north. He caught the star in mid-air, swallowed it up like a truffle and ran away as fast as his trotters could carry him.

"Little pig! What on earth are you doing?" called young Dawn, after him.

But the little pig pretended not to hear her. He sped back to earth at top pig-speed and very soon vanished from view.

What could she do? Dawn would have gone after him there and then, but first she absolutely had to finish taking the stars down from the sky, for the horizon was already growing paler in the east. She got back to her work and only when she had finished did she set out in search of the Pole Star.

From sunrise until midday, she criss-crossed Asia. But nobody there had seen the little pig. From midday until four o'clock, she combed the continent of Africa.

But the little pig had not been seen there either. From four o'clock, she searched all over Europe.

Meanwhile, knowing Dawn would be looking for him, the little pig had taken refuge in France, in a city called... —Well, what was that city called?—Oh yes! A city called Paris. And while scurrying all over Paris, he happened to turn into a street called... —What *was* that street called, now?—Yes, of course: rue Broca! And, on reaching a shop at number 69 rue Broca, the pig vanished into its open door. This was the cafe-grocer's belonging to...—Oh dear, my memory! Who did it belong to?—Oh, yes. To Papa Sayeed!

Papa Sayeed was not there. Nor was Mama Sayeed. Both of them were out, I don't know why. What's more, their eldest daughter Nadia had been stolen away by the wicked witch of rue Mouffetard, and her younger brother Bashir had gone to save her. So now the only people left to look after the shop were the Sayeeds' two youngest daughters: Malika and Rashida.

There the two girls were, enjoying the early-afternoon peace and quiet, when a gust of wind suddenly blew through the shop and, along with it tumbled a little pig—a rather pretty little pig, in fact, whose tightly stretched skin gave out a delicate pink glow (from the star that was glowing inside his tummy). The little pig begged them, breathlessly:

"Save me! Please, save me!"

"What should we save you from?" asked Malika.

"From a little girl! From young Dawn! She's coming after me! She wants to kill me! And eat me whole!"

"No way!" gasped Rashida.

"She does, she does! She's been chasing me since morning! If you don't hide me, she will eat me up!"

And fat tears began to roll down the little pig's cheeks.

The two girls looked at each other.

"Poor thing," said Malika.

"We must do something!" Rashida decided.

"What if we hide him in the cellar?" suggested Malika.

"That's a good idea!"

They sent the little pig down into the cellar and were about to close the trapdoor when he stopped them for a moment:

"Now, if anyone asks for me, you haven't seen me. Understood?"

"All right!" said Malika.

"Oh, and I was forgetting: young Dawn will doubtless tell you some yawn of a shaggy-dog story about some star she'll say I've eaten... Obviously, it's total nonsense: little pigs do not eat stars. I hope you won't believe her for a moment..."

"Of course not!" said Rashida.

"And one more thing! Don't tell your parents about me, it's better if you don't... Parents, you know, they're rather stupid, they don't understand how life works..."

"Okay!" said the two girls, together.

And they let the trapdoor fall closed. Then they looked at each other:

"Why doesn't he want us to tell our parents?" whispered Malika, anxiously. "There's something funny about him!"

"And why does he glow in the dark like that?" asked Rashida. "Did you see him there, in the cellar, while he was talking to us? He looked like a lamp with a pink lampshade!"

Malika scrunched her nose up: she was thinking.

"Perhaps his story about the star is true, after all..."

"But then, are we wrong to hide him?" asked Rashida, very worried.

"Never mind." said Malika. "We should have thought of that before! Now we've taken him in, we can't betray him."

At about five o'clock that afternoon, young Dawn walked into the shop.

"Hello, young ladies! You wouldn't, by any chance, have seen a little pink pig today, would you?"

"Pink all over and glowing like a nightlight?" asked Malika.

"Just like that!"

"No, we haven't seen him!"

"In that case, I'm sorry to disturb you," said young Dawn. "Goodbye, ladies!"

And she left the shop. But five minutes later, she was back:

"Forgive me, ladies. It's about this little pig... If you haven't seen him, how do you know that he glows?"

"It's because he has eaten a star," replied Rashida.

"Indeed he has! Have you seen him, then?"

"No, never!"

"Oh. Right."

And young Dawn left the shop for the second time. Hardly had she stepped outside when she stopped and frowned, then went back into the shop:

"Forgive me, ladies, it's me again... Are you really completely sure that you haven't seen the little pig?"

"Oh yes, quite sure! Absolutely sure!" chorused Malika and Rashida, blushing as pink as pink roses.

Young Dawn gazed at them doubtfully, but since she had no proof, she did not dare challenge them again and so off she went once more, for good this time.

At six o'clock in the evening, Papa and Mama Sayeed came home. They asked the girls:

"Any news from the shop today?"

"Yes!" they said. "Nadia was taken away by the wicked witch."

"Oh? And then?"

"Then Bashir went to save her."

"Oh, good! Anything else?"

"No, nothing else..."

"Very good. Go and have your tea."

A few hours later, the day was almost over. Poor Dawn had searched the whole world but had no luck, and already it was time for her to start pinning the animals who lived in the sky back up there. She picked up her sack of stars, called all the heavenly animals and began to pin them all up again. When she got to the Little Bear, she pinned him up as best she could with the stars she had left, and she was about to go on, when Little Bear stopped her:

"Well? What about my Pole Star? You're forgetting my Pole Star!"

"Drat!" hissed young Dawn into Little Bear's ear. "I think I've lost it. But don't tell anyone. I promise I'll find it for you before tomorrow evening..."

But the Little Bear didn't hear very well in that ear. She began to cry:

"Waaah! My Pole Star! Waah! I want my Pole Star! Waaaaah! The little girl has lost my Pole Star..."

She was making such a racket that the Moon hurried over:

"What's all this? What's going on?"

Very ashamed, young Dawn told her mother what had happened.

"Why didn't you tell me before?"

"I didn't dare, Mama... I thought I could find the star by myself."

"Oh well, that wasn't very clever, was it! Now we shall have to tell your father! And he does not like being woken up, does your father, once he has gone to bed!"

Poor young Dawn finished her work with her

mother helping, sniffing as she went. When they were finished, they went to wake up the Sun.

That night—a beautiful, clear night—there was no Pole Star, but instead a great black space in the sky. And a great many ships that had set out for America ended up in Africa or even in Australia, because they had lost track of where north was.

"Oh, very clever!" grumbled the Sun in a thunderous voice, throwing flames in all directions. "What in heaven can I have done to deserve such a little idiot... I don't know what's stopping me from—"

"Now, now, don't get so worked up," said the Moon, impatiently. "What good will it do?"

"True," admitted the Sun. "But all the same."

Then, turning to young Dawn, he asked:

"Look, what is it that happened, exactly? Tell me everything."

And, when young Dawn had finished her tale, he said:

"That little pig is doubtless hiding at Papa Sayeed's shop. Those little girls must have hidden him. Quick, bring me my great black cloak, my black hat, my black scarf, my black mask and my dark glasses, and I'll be there in a flash."

The Sun put on his great black cloak, his black hat, his black scarf, his black mask and his dark glasses. Dressed like this, no one could tell that he was in fact the Sun. He went down to earth and straight away to see Papa Sayeed.

When he stepped into the shop, Papa Sayeed asked:

"What will it be for monsieur?"

"Nothing," said the Sun. "I would like to talk to you."

Hearing this, Papa Sayeed took him for a door-to-door salesman:

"In that case," he said, "you can come back tomorrow! Why do you always come at this time? You can see that I have customers to serve!"

"I am not who you think I am," said the Sun. "I have come to look for the little pig that has eaten the Pole Star."

"What kind of a tall tale is this? There's no little pig here!"

"And I," said the Sun, "I am certain that there is. Your children let him in."

Papa Sayeed called in his four children, who were watching television:

"Now, what's this story I'm hearing about you? Have any of you four seen a little pig today?"

Nadia said: "I wasn't here during the day—the witch stole me away."

"Me neither," said Bashir, "I went to save Nadia."

But Malika and Rashida stood there in silence, looking at the floor. Papa Sayeed asked:

"And what about you two, now? Have you seen a little pig?"

"A little pig?" asked Malika, in a small voice.

"A little pig?" echoed Rashida.

Papa Sayeed lost his temper.

"Yes, a little pig! Not a hippopotamus, to be sure! Have you both gone deaf?"

"Have you seen a little pig?" Malika asked Rashida.

"Me? Oh no!" Rashida replied. "And you? Have you seen one, a little pig?"

"No, me neither. Not one little pig..."

"Really!" said the Sun. "Are you sure? A little pig, green all over, being chased by an old gentleman with a wooden leg?"

"That's not right!" said Malika indignantly. "He was pink!"

"Besides," added Rashida excitedly, "it wasn't an

237

old gentleman following him: it was a little girl! And she didn't have a wooden leg!"

Just then, they both went quiet, looked at each other and blushed right up to their ears, realizing that they had given each other away.

"There's our proof!" cried the Sun.

"What does this mean?" Papa Sayeed shouted. "Hiding a little pig in my shop—and what's more, without asking! And trying to lie to me, on top of everything!"

The two little girls began to cry:

"But it's not our fault!"

"We thought we were doing the right thing!"

"He begged us so hard!"

"He pleaded with us!"

"He told us the little girl was going to kill him!"

"Kill him and eat him!"

"Enough lies!" thundered Papa Sayeed. "Come here and let me give you each a good smacking."

But this time, the Sun stepped in.

"Don't smack them, Monsieur Sayeed, I am sure they are telling the truth. I know this little pig: he's a terrible liar and quite capable of telling them all this nonsense."

Then, turning to the two girls, he asked them gently:

"And where have you put him?"

"In the cellar," whispered Malika.

"Would you mind showing me your cellar?" the Sun asked Papa Sayeed.

"Well... I would rather not!" said Papa Sayeed. "I don't much like this kind of thing, myself. And besides, it could cause me problems in the future. I don't even know who you are."

"I am the Sun," said the Sun.

"Then, prove it. Take off your dark glasses!"

"I really can't," said the Sun. "If I take them off, the whole house will catch fire!"

"All right then, keep them on," said Papa Sayeed. "And stay back behind the counter."

He lifted the trapdoor. All the customers in the cafe who had been listening to the conversation crowded over to see. As soon as the trapdoor was raised, a soft pink light shone out.

"He's in there!" cried the Sun.

And, without even asking for the ladder, he stretched out one long, *long* arm, lifted the little pig out by his ear and sat him on the marble shop counter. The little pig wriggled and struggled and yelled as loud as he could:

"Let me go! Let me go! I want to stay here!"

"You can stay where you like," said the Sun, "but I want my star back."

"Star? What star? I don't know any star. I've never even seen a star!"

"Liar!" said the Sun. "I can see it shining right through your tummy!"

The little pig looked down at his tummy, saw the glow and gave up pretending:

"All right—take your star, then." he said. "I don't want anything to do with your star! I never wanted it in the first place! I didn't mean to eat it."

"Don't talk so much," said the Sun, "and spit it out, if you can."

The little pig tried and tried to spit out the star, but he couldn't.

"We'll have to make him throw up," said the Sun.

"I have an idea," said Papa Sayeed.

He took a very big glass and in it he put: coffee, mustard, salt, grenadine syrup, rum, pastis, brandy and beer. The little pig gulped down this horrible mixture, went quite pale and began to vomit up everything inside him—except for the star.

At three in the morning, they sent for a vet, who gave the little pig a purgative meant for horses, hoping they might get the star out by the pig's other end. Between four and five o'clock, the little pig did quite a few things, but still no star came out.

When the clock struck half-past five in the morning, the Sun cried:

"It's too bad! I can't wait any longer. The day is dawning and soon I will have to rise—we shall have to use extreme measures! Monsieur Sayeed, can you bring me a knife?"

Papa Sayeed, who was also getting rather fed up, took out the long knife he used for cutting bunches of bananas. The Sun seized it and, without a moment's hesitation, he sank the knife into the little pig's back, making a large cut. Then he slipped two fingers into the slit, drew out the Pole Star and put it in his pocket. The little pig was weeping, but he didn't make a squeak: he may have been a dreadful liar, but he was, all the same, a very brave little pig.

"Thank you, Monsieur Sayeed," said the Sun. "And please accept my apologies for this sleepless night. Now I have to go, for young Dawn has already begun taking the stars down from the sky. I really don't know how to reward your kindness..."

"Well, I know," said Papa Sayeed. "Just keep shining as hotly as you can, so that my customers are thirsty and my business goes well..."

"Right, it's a deal, I'll do my best!"

Then, turning to the little pig, the Sun added:

"As for your punishment, since you so enjoy eating shiny things, you shall be turned into a piggy bank. You shall keep that slot in your back, Monsieur Sayeed will drop his tips in there, and you won't walk free until you're filled up with coins!"

"Great!" said the little pig. "I'll soon be full!"

"There's an optimist!" said the Sun.

Now, the Sun uttered a magic spell. The little pig stopped moving: he had changed into a piggy bank.

The cafe's customers all leant in to look at the piggy bank. As they did so, the Sun skipped out of the door and flew away. Straight away, everyone, including the children, crowded into the street, to watch him go... Within a few seconds, he had vanished from view.

That day turned out rather overcast, for the Sun was a little tired. But from the day after onwards, the

Pole Star shone in the sky once more, and the ships that set out for America mostly arrived in America.

As for the little pig, the Sun had been right to doubt that he would be free very soon. Naturally, customers often leave tips. Naturally, Papa Sayeed never forgets to drop the coins into the piggy bank's slot. But since the children come and shake them out again, I won't say every day, but maybe several times a day, there is reason to fear that the little pig may never again be entirely full up!

The Fool and His Wise Wife

There was once a rich merchant who had three sons. The two older sons were clever but the third one was a fool—and really he was *so* stupid that he was known throughout the land as *Outtaluck*. Every time he was carrying something, he would drop it. Every time he opened his mouth, he would say something stupid. Every time he picked up a tool, he would have an accident. And the people roundabout, who knew him well, preferred to give him food for free than risk letting him do any kind of work.

One fine day, the merchant called his three sons together and said to them:

"Now that you are grown up, you must learn the business of commerce. I am going to give each of you one hundred gold pieces with which to buy some goods, and a ship so you can go and sell your goods abroad."

"Will Outtaluck get this gold too?" asked the two older sons.

"Outtaluck too."

"But he's a hopeless fool!"

"Fool or not, he is still my son, and he shall be treated exactly the same as you two!"

So the merchant gave a hundred gold coins to each of his sons and then they each went into town to buy some goods to sell abroad. Having risen early, the eldest boy was the first to arrive in town. He bought some fine, thick furs and filled his ship with them. Next to arrive was the second son, who filled his ship with a cargo of sweet honey. As for Outtaluck, he got up on the dot of midday, had a relaxed lunch, and set off around two o'clock in the afternoon. Before he had even reached the town, he came across a group of children who had caught a cat and were trying to stuff it into a sack.

"Why are you doing that?" asked the foolish son.

"So we can drown it in the sack," replied the children.

"But why do you want to drown the cat?"

"Because it will be funny."

Outtaluck felt sorry for the cat. He said to the children:

"Don't do that. Give the cat to me."

"No, no!" shouted the children. "We want to drown it. It'll be more fun!"

"So, sell it to me!"

"How much money will you give us for it?"

"I don't know. How much do you want?"

"That depends. How much money do you have here now?"

"I have a hundred gold pieces."

"All right then, give them to us and the cat is yours."

Without arguing, the fool gave the children all his hundred gold pieces and took the cat.

When the three brothers were home again, their father asked:

"What have you each bought with your hundred pieces of gold?"

His eldest son said, "I have bought furs."

"And I," said the second son, "I bought honey."

"And I," said Outtaluck, "I bought this cat that some children wanted to drown."

Hearing this, the two older boys began to laugh helplessly.

"Oh, Outtaluck, that's just like you! A hundred gold pieces for a single cat!"

"Never mind," said their father. "What's done is done. He shall go to sea and he'll sell his cat, just as you will sell the things you have bought."

The merchant blessed his three sons and, the following morning, each one set out in his own ship. They sailed and sailed, and after three months they all arrived at an island that was not on their maps.

Now, there wasn't a single cat on this island. Therefore mice were swarming everywhere, as numerous as blades of grass in the fields, nibbling at everything, making holes in everything, devouring everything. It was a civic disaster.

The oldest brother landed there one evening, planning to take his furs to the local market. But the next morning, when he wanted to sell them, he found they were full of holes, for the mice had nibbled at them during the night.

The second brother landed on the island next, he

too planning to take his merchandise—honey—to the local market. But the following morning, his honey barrels had all sprung holes, the honey had leaked out onto the ground, and it was full of mouse poo.

On the third day, the foolish brother landed with his cat on a leash. Hardly had he reached the island's marketplace, when his cat set about hunting down the mice. He killed ten, twenty, a hundred of them; it was a real massacre. The local merchants came to ask the fool:

"Will you sell us your wonderful animal? How much do you want for him?"

"I don't know," said Outtaluck. "How much will you give me?"

"We can offer you three barrels of gold."

"Well then, it's a deal!"

The foolish brother gave the merchants his cat and received three barrels of gold from them in return. Then, seeing his brothers looking at him strangely, he said:

"Come now, brothers, don't be sad! Why don't you each take a barrel of gold with you and I'll stay here with the one that's left?"

"Thank you," said the brothers, "but why should

we leave you here? Won't you come home to our father's house, then?"

"No," replied Outtaluck. "I'm very happy here. It's the only place where no one has yet called me a fool."

"All right, goodbye then!"

"Goodbye!"

And the two older brothers left, each in his own ship with his barrel of gold. Outtaluck stayed behind with the third barrel.

"Now what on earth can I do with this thing?" he wondered. "I've no need for all this gold..."

He gave his gold away among the poor of the island, then he sold his ship and with the money he bought some incense. He piled all the incense into a great heap on the beach. When it grew dark, Outtaluck set fire to the heap of incense and, while it crackled away, he danced around it chanting:

"This is for you, sweet God! This is for you, kind God!"

Hearing this, an angel floated down from the sky in a column of smoke and said:

"Many thanks, Outtaluck! As a reward, I am required to give you the next thing that you ask for. What is it that you want?"

At this, our fool was rather embarrassed.

"What I want? But what *do* I want? I haven't a clue! I've never thought about it."

"Listen," said the angel, kindly, "take your time, go for a walk and ask the first three people you meet for some advice."

"Thank you, thank you, Mister Angel," replied the fool.

And off he went. After just a few steps, he came across a sailor:

"Here, sailor, would you mind giving me some advice? An angel has asked me what I want. What should I reply?"

The sailor began to laugh:

"What do I know! I'm not in your shoes!"

But, seeing that the sailor was making fun of him, Outtaluck grew angry:

"Oh, it's like that is it?" he said.

And *paff*! With one punch he cracked the sailor's head open.

A little farther on, he came across a peasant.

"Could you tell me, peasant: an angel has asked me what I want. What do you think I should reply?"

The peasant too began to laugh:

"Ask for whatever you like. It's none of my business, to be sure!"

At these words, the fool grew even angrier than before:

"Isn't it really, now?"

And *boff*! He killed the peasant with a single punch.

Farther on again, he came to an old lady:

"Tell me grandmother, I'm in a bit of a spot. An angel has asked me what I want..."

The old lady looked at him. She understood right away that he wasn't very smart. So she replied seriously:

"That is a tough one, indeed. You could, of course, ask for wealth... But if you became too rich, you might forget about God... If I were you, I would ask for a wise wife."

"Thank you, kind old lady!"

And our fool went back to the beach. The heap of incense was still glowing red, and the angel was still floating there above it in the smoke.

"So, Outtaluck, what is it that you want?"

"I want a wise wife!"

"Excellent!" said the angel. "You have made a very

good choice. Go for a walk in the woods tomorrow morning and you shall find her."

And the angel went back up to heaven.

The next morning, the fool walked out into the nearest forest. He walked there for a long, long time without meeting anybody. Then, all of a sudden, he heard a voice pleading, from behind a bush:

"Don't kill me! Please don't kill me!"

He leant over to look—it was a wounded dove, her feathers spotted with blood, hopping about on one foot and whimpering:

"Don't kill me! Don't kill me!"

"I hadn't the least thought of killing you!" said the fool.

"Then take me in your arms," begged the dove.

"I haven't got time," the fool replied. "There's someone I have to meet, you know..."

But the dove said again, pleading:

"Please! Take me in your arms, hold me in your arms..."

Outtaluck took pity on her. He picked up the dove and cradled her gently, then he kissed her little head.

The dove said to him:

"That's lovely. Again, please. And when I go to sleep, tap my right wing once lightly with your finger."

Outtaluck kept on stroking her. After a minute, the dove closed her eyes and her bill began to droop forward. Then the fool gave her right wing a little tap with his finger and... no longer was he holding a bird in his arms but a superb young woman, who began to sing:

You it was who caught me
You who knew to keep me
And you may have me for your wife—for ever.

Outtaluck was delighted, but also a little ashamed of himself, at the same time:

"Alas," he said, "I can see that you are wise and beautiful, but I have no profession by which to earn a living for us; indeed, everywhere I am known as Outtaluck."

The young lady laughed, kissed him and answered:

"From today, no one will call you Outtaluck ever again; instead they'll call you Lucky Devil!"

"You're kind," said the fool, "but I have to warn you: I don't even know where we can sleep tonight!"

"No matter! Let's walk straight on ahead."

They went straight on, letting their feet carry them forward. When night fell, they stopped beneath a tree, and the wife said to her husband:

"Say your prayers and go to sleep. Tomorrow is another day."

The fool said his prayers, lay down and went to sleep. As soon as he was asleep, the young wife took a book of magic spells out of her bodice, opened it and read aloud:

> *Mother's servants, if you can*
> *Come, help me and my new man*

Straight away, two giants appeared:

"Daughter of your mother, what do you want from us?"

"I want you to build me a fabulous palace, with everything I might need: servants, furniture, a chapel and a cellar: everything, please!"

"Daughter of your mother, you can count on us!"

*

The following morning, when the fool woke up, he was lying in an enormous bed, in the finest room of a magnificent palace. A dozen servants came in to serve him his breakfast. Turning over, he saw that his wife was lying next to him. He asked her:

"What is happening to us?"

"Oh, it's nothing," she yawned. "I couldn't sleep during the night, so I did this to distract myself."

The fool gazed at her admiringly:

"You really are wise!" he said.

She giggled:

"You haven't seen anything yet! For now, hurry and have your breakfast. When you've finished, you must come and see the King to say sorry for building our palace in his kingdom."

The fool had a tasty breakfast, then he got dressed and was taken by horse-drawn carriage to the kingdom's capital city, where he went to see the King.

"What do you want from me?" asked the King.

"I have come to apologize, Your Majesty."

"Apologize? Apologize for what?"

"For building my palace on your land."

"Hmm!" the King pondered. "It's not a very serious offence... But since you are here, show me this palace of yours! I am curious to see it, all the same..."

"Of course, Your Majesty."

The fool brought the King along in the carriage to see his home. When the King saw the palace from outside, he gawped in amazement. When he saw inside it, he gasped in wonder. But when he saw the fool's wife, he grew sad and couldn't say another word, for he had fallen in love.

Seeing the King come back home, his mother asked him:

"Why are you so melancholy, my child?"

"Ah!" sighed the King. "It's because I have such wicked thoughts!"

"What thoughts?"

"I saw the fool's wife and I fell in love with her there and then! I think it's unfair that that woman does not belong to me."

"In that case," said the old Queen Mother, "we shall have to steal her from him!"

"Yes, but how? They are married!"

"Listen," said the Queen Mother, "I have an idea: give him something to do for you, something very,

very difficult. And when he can't do it, well then, you can chop his head off!"

"Now that," said the King, "is a good idea!"

He went to bed, very pleased with his new plan.

The next day, he summoned the fool and said to him:

"Since you have built this beautiful palace, I have an order for you: you shall build an avenue to link your palace with mine. This avenue must be paved with gold. The trees lining it must have an emerald for every leaf and a ruby for every fruit. In every tree, there must be a pair of nesting firebirds, singing all the songs of Paradise. And at the foot of every tree there must be a pair of seafaring cats miaowing along in time with the birds. Let all this be ready by tomorrow morning, otherwise I shall cut off your head!"

The fool went back to his palace home, very downcast. His wife asked:

"Well, what's up?"

"Ooh, I don't want to talk about it," the fool replied.

He told his wife what the King had said. She laughed out loud:

"Is that all? But this will be a piece of cake! Off you go now, say your prayers and get to bed: tomorrow is another day."

The fool went to bed. As soon as he was asleep, his wife stepped outside the palace, took the magic-spell book from her bodice, opened it and began to read:

Mother's servants, if you can
Come, help me and my new man

The next morning, the King took a look out of his window and, to his great surprise, he saw the avenue paved with gold linking the two palaces, with the emerald- and ruby-bearing trees, the singing firebirds and the cats all miaowing in time. He called his mother over:

"Look, mother! The fool is cleverer than you thought. He has built us an avenue paved with gold in a single night!"

"Hmm!" harrumphed the Queen Mother, with a mean smile. "It isn't he who is clever, it's his wife! But don't despair: I have another idea. Order the fool to go into the next world, to ask the old King, your own dead father's soul, where he hid his gold. It will be impossible for him to get there, and then of course you can cut off his head!"

"A brilliant idea!" said the King.

That very day, he commanded the fool:

"Since you are so clever, pop over to the next world and ask my father's soul where he hid his gold. And if you can't find the gold for me, don't bother coming back!

The fool went back home and told his wife what the King had said. She laughed until her sides hurt.

"A fine plan indeed!" she said. "This time we have some work to do. Right, come with me."

She took a magic ball out of her bodice and threw it in front of her. The ball began to roll along the ground. The fool and his wife followed it. The ball rolled all the way to the sea. The sea divided in front of it and the ball continued to roll along the dry seabed. The fool and his wife kept on following, walking now between two walls of water. They walked and walked, and when at last the ball stopped rolling, they were in the next world.

There they found a very old man with a crown on his head and, on his back, an immense bundle of wood, and behind him, two devils whipping tirelessly at him, to keep him moving.

"It's the King's father," said the fool's wife.

So the fool stepped forward and shouted, "Stop!" to the two devils.

"What do you want?" asked the devils.

"I need to talk to that man!"

"Then who will carry our wood, while he is dallying with you?"

"Just a moment," said the wife.

She took the spell book out of her bodice and called out:

> *Mother's servants, if you can*
> *Come, help me and my new man*

The two giants appeared instantly.

"Daughter of your mother, what do you want from us?"

"Carry these two devils' wood, while we talk with this gentleman."

The two giants picked up the bundle of wood. And

as they did, the old man fell to the ground, quite worn out by his eternal burden. The fool approached him:

"Your son has sent me to you. He would like to know where you have hidden your gold."

"My son?" muttered the old King. "He would do better to stick to governing his country wisely, and to leave my gold alone! Tell him, if he cannot be a better king than I, he will end up just as I have done!"

"Okay," the fool replied, "I'll tell him. But that's not really what he was after. What about the gold?"

The old King sighed deeply, then he pulled out a little key which was hanging on a string around his neck:

"All right, then," he said. "I quite see there's no point trying to teach you living people about right and wrong. So, tell my son to go down into the palace cellar. He will find the door to my treasure trove behind the racks of wine bottles. This is the key to that door."

And the old King gave the fool the key. The fool said thank you, and he and his wife set out on their long way back home. Meanwhile, the devils returned and began, once again, to crack their whips and drive the old King ever onwards.

The next day, the fool went back to the King's palace. The King asked him:

"Haven't you left yet?"

"I have left," the fool replied, "and I've come back too. I met Your Majesty's father."

"You met him? Where?"

"In the next world, Your Majesty."

"And what is he up to there?"

"He carries wood for some devils there," said the fool, "and the devils whip him to make him go faster."

The King made a sour face. This kind of thing is never very nice to hear, especially, as was the case now, in front of the whole royal court. The King looked down and asked the fool:

"Are you making fun of me?"

"Of course not, Your Majesty!"

"All right. And what did my father say?"

"He said you would do better to stick to governing the country wisely, and to leave his gold alone, if you don't want to end up like him..."

"You're lying!"

"No, I'm not lying, Your Majesty!"

"Well... what about the secret hiding place? Didn't he say anything about where he hid his treasure?"

"He did, Your Majesty. You must go down to the cellar and, behind the racks of wine bottles, you will find a little door, which this little key will open..."

The King snatched the key out of the fool's hand and left the court room, saying:

"I shall go and see right away. And if it isn't true, I will cut off your head!"

He went down to the cellar, pushed aside the racks of bottles, and there he did find a little door. He opened it with the key: it was indeed the door to the old King's treasure trove.

That evening, the King said to his mother:

"The fool is far cleverer than we thought. He has brought me the key to the treasure trove!"

"No he isn't!" said the old Queen Mother. "It's his wife who is clever, not him! But don't worry, I have one more idea: command him to go to Nowhere-land, to find Nowhere-man, and to ask him for *je-ne-sais-quoi*. *This* time he won't come back and you'll be able to take his wife!"

"What a brilliant idea!" exclaimed the King, thrilled. The next morning he called the fool and commanded him:

"Off you go, to Nowhere-land, where you must

find Nowhere-man and ask him to give you *je-ne-sais-quoi*. If you are unlucky enough to come back without it, I will have your head cut off.

And, just as the fool was leaving, the King added:

"Oh—I almost forgot. You must leave your wife here. She is banned from going with you."

For the third time, the fool went home and told his wife what the King had said. This time, his wife looked thoughtful:

"This one," she said, "this one is a real toughie. And you have to go alone..."

She thought for a long time, then she gave her husband an embroidered towel, saying:

"Listen carefully. You must leave here and keep on walking straight ahead until you reach the end of the earth. In every place you stop along the way, ask to take a bath. And only dry yourself with this towel, which I embroidered myself!"

Then she took the magic-spell book from her bodice and read aloud:

> *Mother's servants, if you can*
> *Come, help me and my new man*

"Daughter of your mother, what do you want from us?" asked the two giants.

"As soon as my husband has left," she said, "transform this palace into a mountain and me into a rock on the mountain. That way the King won't be able to do anything to me."

The fool kissed his wife, then, taking the towel, he went on his way. After just a few steps, he turned round to look, and what did he see? Instead of his palace he saw a tall mountain, and instead of his wife, he saw a rock.

On he went, straight ahead, going wherever his feet led him, for days, weeks and months. He crossed a sea, then another land, then yet another sea, then other lands and seas... so far and for so long that one day he found himself at the end of the earth. Before him was nothing but a river of fire. And beside the river stood a little house.

He looked inside the little house and there, in the middle of the living room, sitting in a great armchair, he found an ancient witch who instantly began to sniff the air:

"Pouf! Pouf! There's a smell of Christians in here!"

"Excuse me, Granny," said the fool, "but I'm looking for a place called 'Nowhere-land'."

"You've no need to look any further," said the old crone, "for I shall eat you here and now!"

"Well! As you wish," said the fool. "But may I take a bath first?"

"Certainly!" said the old witch. "That will save my having to wash you myself."

She let him run a hot bath. The fool washed and, when he had finished, she handed him a towel.

"Here—dry yourself off."

"No thanks," he said, "I have my own towel."

And he took out his embroidered towel. When she saw the towel, the old witch was astonished. She asked:

"Where did you take that towel from?"

"I didn't take it from anywhere. My wife embroidered it."

"Your wife? But in that case... you have married my daughter! Only she and I can embroider in that way... Come to my arms, my son-in-law!"

And the old lady hugged and kissed the fool. Then she asked:

"But what are you doing coming all the way here?"

The fool told her his whole story: about his two clever brothers, his champion cat, the angel, the injured dove and the King's commands.

"Tell me, Mother, do you know of a place called Nowhere-land?"

"No," said the old lady, "never heard of it. But wait a moment, I'll go and find out more!"

She went outside, where she stood facing the forest and called as loudly as she could:

"Beasts of the forest, come to me!"

Instantly, all the beasts in the forest came to her:

"Old lady at the end of the earth," they chorused, "what do you want from us?"

"Do you know the place called Nowhere-land?"

"No, we don't know it."

"All right. Off you go, then."

The beasts went back into the forest. Then the old lady raised her arms up and called as loudly as she could:

"Birds in the sky, come to me!"

Then the sky went black all over, and all the birds in the entire world came to perch around the witch:

"Old lady at the end of the earth," they chirped, "what do you want from us?"

"Do you know the place called Nowhere-land?"

"No, we don't know it."

"Never mind. Goodbye, then, till next time!"

And the birds all flew away. At the same time, the fool began to weep:

"Nobody knows this place! I shall never see my country—or my wife—again!"

"Now, now, you big baby, don't cry!" said the old lady, kindly. "We still haven't asked the fish."

She took him to the seashore. There she began to call:

"Fish of the salt seas and fish of the fresh waters, come to me!"

At once all the fish in the world were teeming in the sea at their feet. The old lady asked:

"Do you know the place called Nowhere-land?"

"Nope!" replied the fish.

"Never mind. Goodbye!"

The old witch brought the fool back home with her. This time, the fool was so miserable that he even forgot to cry. And the old lady also said nothing.

When they were nearly there, they heard a peculiar voice croaking from behind them.

"What, what, what?"

They span around. It was a frog which was hopping after them.

"What, what, what?"

The old lady asked:

"What do *you* want?"

The frog replied:

"Excuse me; I'm terribly late. I only just heard that you had called for all the beasts in the forest..."

"And where were you when I called?" asked the old witch.

"I," the frog said, "I was in a place called Nowhereland. Do you know it?"

"Really? That's lucky," said the old lady. "Would you mind taking my son-in-law there with you?"

"At your service! Have him climb on my back."

With these words, the frog began to swell and swell. Soon she had grown as big as a man. The fool sat on her as if she were a horse. He just had time to call to the old witch:

"Thank you so much, little Mother!"

And *hop*! The frog leapt over the river of fire. On the other side, she said to her rider:

"Now you can get down. We have reached Nowhere-land. Don't worry about your return

journey: when you have found what you're looking for, you won't need me any longer."

And *hop*! She made a leap and disappeared.

Now the fool was all by himself, in the midst of an empty, rocky land. He walked for a while, until he came across a big house. He went inside and looked all over it, poking his nose into every room, but... nobody was home! Just as he was about to leave, he heard the sound of steps in the entrance hall. Quickly, he hid inside a cupboard in the great hall, and peeked out through a gap in the door. The person who entered was a stately old man who sat down on a chair and called:

"Nowhere-man!"

A voice called back:

"Yes, my lord?"

"I am hungry. Set the table!"

A table appeared, covered with good things to eat and drink. The old man ate and drank his fill, then he called again:

"Nowhere-man!"

"Yes, my lord?"

"I have finished. Clear the table!"

And just as quickly, the table disappeared. Now

the stately old man stood up and left the room. As soon as he had gone, our fool stepped out of his hiding place, sat on a chair and, in his turn, called out:

"Nowhere-man, are you there?"

"Yes, I'm here."

"I am hungry. Set the table."

And the table returned, covered in good things. The fool was about to begin eating when he had another idea:

"Nowhere-man, are you still there?"

"Yes, I'm still here."

"Then come and sit down too, and dine with me."

"Thank you kindly," said the voice, trembling. "I have served this old man for thousands of years but not once has he invited me to his table. You thought of it straight away. Well, in return, from now on I shall never leave your side!"

At this, they both sat down to eat. While the fool ate, he saw food rise and vanish from the table, bottles that poured themselves and glasses that emptied themselves in mid-air. When he had eaten his fill, he asked:

"Nowhere-man, are you still hungry?"

"No, Master, I've had enough."

"Then clear the table!"

The table disappeared.

"Nowhere-man, are you still there?"

"As I said, I shall never leave your side again!"

"Do you think you could give me *je-ne-sais-quoi*?"

"But of course, right away, sir. Here you are!"

At that moment, something quite extraordinary happened. Nothing had changed and yet everything was different. The fool breathed more freely, his blood flowed more rapidly. He saw the world around him as if he had opened his eyes for the very first time. He found everything beautiful, everything fine; he understood everything, he loved everything. He felt strong, free, joyous and filled with crazy high spirits. Standing there by himself, he began to laugh:

"But it's true!" he exclaimed. "You have given me a little *je-ne-sais-quoi*..."

"Would you like anything else?" asked the voice.

"Yes, please," said the fool. "Can you take me home?"

"Right away. Don't be afraid!"

That very second, the fool found himself being lifted into the air and now he was flying, but so fast, so very fast, that he lost his cap!

"Hey there, Nowhere-man, stop! I've lost my cap!"

But the voice replied:

"I'm sorry, Master, but your cap is now twenty thousand miles away! It is gone. There's no point looking for it now!"

A second later, the fool slowed to a halt in front of a craggy great mountain and then came down to land beside a large rock. He hardly had time to see where he was before the mountain turned back into his palace and the rock became his wife, once again. She ran to kiss him:

"Did you find what you were looking for, my darling?"

"Just a moment!" answered the fool.

And he called:

"Nowhere-man!"

"Yes, Master!"

"Can you give a little *je-ne-sais-quoi* to my wife, too?"

"Right away, master! There you go, ma'am!"

And instantly, his wife began to laugh:

"So it's true! You really have given me a little *je-ne-sais-quoi*... Now let's go and see the King!"

They took their coach and set out along the

gold-paved avenue. On both sides the trees tinkled, the birds sang and the cats miaowed. They soon arrived at the royal palace and were shown into the throne room.

"You again!" growled the King. "What are you doing here?"

The fool replied:

"I've been to Nowhere-land, where I found Nowhere-man, and he gave me some *je-ne-sais-quoi*. Wouldn't you like some too?"

"Well, I suppose I would," said the King. "I'm curious to know..."

But he abruptly broke off what he was saying—and then burst out laughing:

"So it's true after all! You really have given me a little *je-ne-sais-quoi*!"

Then he called:

"Mother! Mother!"

The old Queen Mother came in.

"Listen mother: the fool has returned and he has given me some *je-ne-sais-quoi*. Would you like to try some too?"

"Absolutely not!" said the Queen Mother. "What is this nonsense?"

"Go on, Nowhere-man, give her some anyway!" the fool asked his servant.

But the voice replied:

"I can't, I'm afraid: if she will not accept it, I cannot give it to her."

"Now, my dear fool," said the King, "keep your wife and stay near me, from now on. As I have no children, you shall be King when I am gone."

So it came about that, to this day, everyone in the kingdom is happy. Everyone except for the Queen Mother, who is just as dismal, mean and sad as ever. But she consoles herself with the thought that she at least still has her wits about her, while the others are all mad, every single one of them.

Afterword

Children understand everything—as everybody knows. If I knew that children would be the only ones reading this book, I would not even think of writing an afterword. But, alas, I'm afraid that these tales will be read as much by grown-ups as by younger people. So I feel I should provide a few explanations.

Rue Broca is not a street quite like any other street. If you look at a map of Paris, you will see—or think you see—that rue Pascal and rue Broca cross the boulevard de Port-Royal at right angles. If, confident in your map-reading, you were to take your car and drive down this boulevard, expecting then to turn into one or other of these two side streets, you might go back and forth a hundred times between the Observatory at one end of the boulevard and

Gobelins station at the other, but you would not find either of those two streets.

So, you will ask me: are rue Broca and rue Pascal made-up streets? Not at all! They do exist. And they do indeed run, in nearly straight lines, from boulevard Arago to rue Claude-Bernard. Therefore, they ought to cross the boulevard de Port-Royal.

The explanation of this anomaly is not to be found on your map, for the map can only show two dimensions. As in Einstein's world, at this spot, the surface of Paris curves and passes right over itself, so to speak. Forgive me for drawing on the jargon of science fiction, but really, there is no other way to say this: as with rue Pascal, rue Broca forms a dent, a hollow, a dive into three-dimensional sub-space.

Now, leave your car in its garage and return to the boulevard de Port-Royal, but this time on foot. Set out from Gobelins station and forge ahead, along whichever pavement you prefer. At a certain point, you will see that the row of houses that lines the boulevard has a gap in it. Instead of marching along beside shops or the wall of an apartment building as usual, you are walking alongside a space, a space fenced off by a railing to stop you falling into it. On the same pavement, not much farther along, you'll see the head of a staircase that appears to plunge deep into the entrails of the earth, like the steps that take you down to the Metro. Go down this staircase without fear. Once at the bottom, you are by no means underground; in fact, you will be in rue Pascal. Above your head, you'll see something that looks like a bridge. This bridge is the boulevard de Port-Royal, which you have just left behind.

A little farther along the boulevard, you will find another such staircase, like the first, but this one leading down to rue Broca.

This is bizarre, but it is true.

Now, let's ignore rue Pascal—it is too straight, too wide, too short also to harbour any mystery—and look at rue Broca alone.

This is a twisty street, narrow, crooked and sunken. By virtue of the spatial anomaly that I have described, although both its ends come out in Paris, the street itself is not quite part of Paris. No distance away, but on another plane, underground yet in the open air, this street by itself forms something like a small village. For the people who live there, this gives it a rather special feeling.

First, everybody knows everybody, and each one of them knows more or less what the others do and what they're busy with, which is exceptional in a city like Paris.

And then, the majority of them come from all kinds of different places; very few are from Paris. In this street, I have met Berbers, Algerian French, Spaniards, Portuguese, Italians, a Pole, a Russian... even a few French people from other parts of France!

Still, the people of rue Broca share at least one common pleasure: they love stories.

I have had many misfortunes in my literary career, the majority of which I attribute to the fact that the French in general—and Parisians in particular—do not like stories. They demand the truth, or, failing that, plausibility, realism. While the only stories that really interest me are those about which I am certain, from the start, that they have never happened, will never happen and could never happen. I feel that, due to the basic fact that it makes no documentary or ideological claims to justify its existence, an impossible tale has every chance of containing a good deal more profound truth in it than any story that is merely plausible.

Which perhaps makes me—I console myself—more of a realist in my own way than all those who claim to seek the truth, and who spend their lives stupidly ruled by insipid lies—lies that are indeed realistic purely by virtue of how insipid they are!

And now—one occasion does not make a habit!—here is a true story:

At number 69, rue Broca (I know, I know! I shall now be accused of God knows what dreadful innuendo. But what can I do? It was at number 69, not 67 or 71. For all you lovers of truth, this is one for you!). As I was saying, then: at number 69, rue Broca, there is a cafe-grocer's, the owner of which, Papa Sayeed, is a Berber married to a Breton woman. At the time of my story, they had four children: three girls and one boy (they had a fifth child later). The eldest girl is called Nadia, the second Malika, the third Rashida, and the little boy, who at the time was the youngest child, is called Bashir. Next to the cafe, there is a mansion house. In this house, among other tenants, lives a certain Monsieur Riccardi, Italian as his name suggests, also the father of four children, of whom the eldest is called Nicolas and the youngest is called Tina. I am leaving out other names, because there's no need for them and they would only be confusing.

Nicolas Riccardi often played in the street with the Sayeed children, for his father was a regular customer at the shop. This had been going on for a while and nobody would have dreamt of writing any of it down in a book had a certain odd character not one day turned up in the area.

This person was known as Monsieur Pierre. He was fairly tall, with chestnut hair that stuck up in spikes like a hedgehog, browny-green eyes and glasses. He always wore a two-day-old beard (people even wondered how he managed to keep his beard in what is usually a very temporary state, for a beard) and his clothes, such as they were, seemed always on the verge of falling apart. He was forty years old, a bachelor, and he lived up above on the boulevard de Port-Royal.

He came to rue Broca only to frequent the cafe, but he was often there and at all hours of the day. Besides, his tastes were modest: he appeared to live mainly on biscuits and chocolate, also on fruit when there was any, and all washed down with a great number of milky coffees and mint teas.

When he was asked what he did, he would reply that he was a writer. As his books were never seen anywhere, especially not in bookshops, this reply satisfied nobody, and for a long time the population of rue Broca wondered what he really did for a living.

When I say the population, I mean the grown-ups. The children never wondered anything of the sort, for they had understood right away: Monsieur Pierre was keeping his cards close; he was not a man like other men, really he was an old witch!

Sometimes, trying to unmask him, they would dance around him calling:

"Witch, old witch with your coconuts!"

Or again:

"Witch, old witch with your rubber jewellery!"

Instantly, Monsieur Pierre would throw off his disguise and become what he really was: he would wrap his old raincoat around his head, leaving only his face uncovered, let his thick glasses slide down to the end of his crooked nose and scowl frightfully. Then he would pounce on the kids, with all his claws out, giving a high, shrill, nasal cackle, something like the bleat of an old nanny goat.

The children would run away as if they were dreadfully afraid—but really they weren't as frightened as all that, for when the witch got hold of any of them, they would wriggle around and beat her off with their fists; and they were quite right to do so, for that is how we should treat old witches. They are only dangerous when we are afraid of them. Unmasked and shown who's in charge, they become rather good fun. At this stage, they can be tamed.

So it was with Monsieur Pierre. Once the children had forced him to reveal his true identity, everyone (starting with Monsieur Pierre himself) was greatly relieved, and normal relations were soon established.

One day when Monsieur Pierre was sitting at a table, enjoying one of his endless milky coffees, with the children clustered around, he began, of his own accord, to tell them a story. The next day, at their request, he told another one, and then on the days that followed, he told still more stories. The more he told, the more the children asked him to tell. Monsieur Pierre was obliged to start rereading all the collections of stories that he had ever read since his own childhood, simply in order to satisfy his audience. He told them stories from Charles Perrault, the tales of Hans Andersen and the Brothers Grimm, Russian stories, Greek, French and Arabic tales... and the children are still asking for them!

After a year and a half, having no more stories left to tell, Monsieur Pierre made the children a proposal: they would all meet every Thursday afternoon and together they would make up brand-new stories. And if they could come up with enough stories, the stories could be put into a book.

Which is what they did, and that is how this collection came about.

The stories in the collection were, thus, not written by Monsieur Pierre alone.* They were improvised by him in collaboration with his listeners—and whoever has not worked in this way may struggle to imagine all that the children could contribute, from solid ideas to poetic discoveries and even dramatic situations, often surprisingly bold ones.

---

*   Apart from 'The Witch in the Broom Cupboard', which is inspired by Russian folklore.

I'll give a few examples, so first of all the first sentences in 'The Pair of Shoes':

"There once was a pair of shoes that got married. The right shoe, which was the man, was called Nicolas, and the left shoe, which was the lady, was called Tina."

These few lines, which form the seed for the story that follows, come from young Nicolas Riccardi, whose little sister's name does indeed happen to be Tina.

Scoobidoo, the doll who knew everything, really existed, as did the guitar that became firm friends with the potato. And even as I write these words, the cunning little pig is still making himself useful as the piggy bank in Papa Sayeed's cafe.

On this same cafe's counter, in 1965, there was also a glass bowl that held two little fish, one red, the other yellow with black spots. It was Bashir who first realized that these fish could be "magic", and this is why they appear in 'The Witch in the Broom Cupboard'.

As for those who will say that these stories are too serious for children, I offer the following reply in advance, with the help of one last example:

In an early version of the tale titled 'Uncle Pierre's House', my ghost only realized that he was a ghost thanks to the little girl amusing herself by putting her hand through his ethereal leg. It was Nadia, Papa Sayeed's eldest daughter, who had the inspired idea of having the little girl sit in the same armchair as the ghost, so that, on waking, the ghost discovers her sitting "right inside Uncle Pierre's tummy". These last few words are Nadia's own. Can grown-ups appreciate the symbolic value and moral beauty of this marvellous image? Our poor old ghost, a perfect specimen of the hardened, shrivelled-up, embittered old bachelor, is suddenly able to see himself as he really is. Suddenly liberty is within his reach, and truth, and generosity; he is—in short—set free, and his new freedom begins from the very moment when he symbolically becomes a mother. My friend Nietzsche also writes, I don't recall exactly where, of men as mothers... Yet it took a little girl to come up with this perfect idea!

But I'll stop here, for it would after all be a bit much if, in a book intended for children, the afterword meant for the adults were itself to take up more space than your average fairy tale!

In any case, I haven't much else to add, except to wish my young friends from rue Broca happy reading, and the same to all who live on other streets in other towns, everywhere.

Pierre Gripari, 1966

Translator's Acknowledgements

I would like to thank Audrey Stanton and Etty Bo Tedman specially for their very helpful reading, also Michelle Stanton and Kerry Bell for their interpretation and comments, and Harold Lewis, who is always a trusty reader.

Pierre Gripari, the Author

Pierre Gripari was born in 1925 in Paris, to a French mother and a Greek father. He studied at the prestigious Louis-le-Grand lycée, and tried his hand at various jobs, including serving in the army and acting as a trade-union delegate for an oil company.

He resigned in 1957 in order to become a writer, but it was not until the 1970s that he became famous, with the publication of his *Contes de la rue Broca*, translated in this volume. In these tales, the giants, witches and mermaids of traditional fairy tales leap from the page, animated by a very modern spirit. Blessed with a healthy disrespect for authority, the author took great pleasure in upsetting the natural order of the fantastic.

Pierre Gripari died in Paris in 1990.

Puig Rosado, the Illustrator

Puig Rosado was born in Spain on April Fools' Day, 1931—a date of birth that is surely not entirely free of responsibility for the course the rest of his life then took. His humorous posters, drawings and cartoons have been published in numerous countries, his work is on display in museums across Europe, and he has been honoured with many prizes. Puig Rosado is absolutely convinced that people with no sense of humour go, without exception, to hell!

PUSHKIN CHILDREN'S BOOKS

Just as we all are, children are fascinated by stories. From the earliest age, we love to hear about monsters and heroes, romance and death, disaster and rescue, from every place and time.

In 2013, we created Pushkin Children's Books to share these tales from different languages and cultures with younger readers, and to open the door to the wide, colourful worlds these stories offer.

From picture books and adventure stories to fairy tales and classics, and from fifty-year-old bestsellers to current huge successes abroad, the books on the Pushkin Children's list reflect the very best stories from around the world, for our most discerning readers of all: children.